GALLUP YOUTH SURVEY: MAJOR ISSUES AND TRENDS

TEENS, HEALTH & OBESITY

Dr. Peter Owens

Developed in Association with the Gallup Organization

TEENS, HEALTH & OBESITY

Dr. Peter Owens

Developed in
Association with the
Gallup Organization

Mason Crest
450 Parkway Drive, Suite D
Broomall, PA 19008
www.masoncrest.com

Printed and bound in the United States of America.

CPSIA Compliance Information: Batch #GYS2013. For further information, contact Mason Crest at 1-866-MCP-Book

First printing
1 3 5 7 9 8 6 4 2

Library of Congress Cataloging-in-Publication Data

Owens, Peter, 1945-
  Teens, health, and obesity / Peter Owens.
      pages cm. — (The Gallup youth survey : major issues and trends)
  Includes bibliographical references and index.
  ISBN 978-1-4222-2961-3 (hc)
  ISBN 978-1-4222-2997-2 (pb)
  ISBN 978-1-4222-8878-8 (ebook)
  1. Youth—Health and hygiene—Juvenile literature. 2. Obesity in adolescence—
Juvenile literature. 3. Eating disorders in adolescence—Juvenile literature.
  I. Title.
  RA564.5.O94 2014
  616.85'2600835—dc23
                              2013007239

The Gallup Youth Survey: Major Issues and Trends series ISBN: 978-1-4222-2948-4

Contents

Introduction

By George Gallup

As the United States moves into the new century, there is a vital need for insight into what it means to be a young person in America. Today's teenagers will be the leaders and shapers of the 21st century. The future direction of the United States is being determined now in their hearts and minds and actions. Yet how much do we as a society know about this important segment of the U.S. populace who have the potential to lift our nation to new levels of achievement and social health?

We need to hear the voices of young people, and to help them better articulate their fears and their hopes. Our youth have much to share with their elders — is the older generation really listening? Is it carefully monitoring the hopes and fears of teenagers today? Failure to do so could result in severe social consequences.

The Gallup Youth Survey was conducted between 1977 and 2006 to help society meet this responsibility to youth, as well as to inform and guide our leaders by probing the social and economic attitudes and behaviors of young people. With theories abounding about the views, lifestyles, and values of adolescents, the Gallup Youth Survey, through regular scientific measurements of teens themselves, served as a sort of reality check.

Surveys reveal that the image of teens in the United States today is a negative one. Teens are frequently maligned, misunderstood, or simply ignored by their elders. Yet over four decades the Gallup Youth Survey provided ample evidence of the very special qualities of the nation's youngsters. In fact, if our society is less racist, less sexist, less polluted, and more peace loving, we can in considerable measure thank our young people, who have been on the leading edge on these issues. And the younger generation is not geared to greed: survey after survey has shown that teens have a keen interest in helping those people, especially in their own communities, who are less fortunate than themselves

Young people have told Gallup that they are enthusiastic about helping others, and are willing to work for world peace and a healthy world. They feel positive about their schools and even more positive about their teachers. A large majority of American teenagers have reported that they are happy and excited about the future, feel very close to their families, are likely to marry, want to have children, are satisfied with their personal lives, and desire to reach the top of their chosen careers.

But young adults face many threats, so parents, guardians, and concerned adults must commit themselves to do everything possible to help tomorrow's parents, citizens, and leaders avoid or overcome risky behaviors so that they can move into the future with greater hope and understanding.

The Gallup Organization is enthusiastic about this partnership with Mason Crest Publishers. Through carefully and clearly written books on a variety of vital topics dealing with teens, Gallup Youth Survey statistics are presented in a way that gives new depth and meaning to the data. The focus of these books is a practical one—to provide readers with the statistics and solid information that they need to understand and to deal with each important topic.

— — —

Memo to teens: Do yourself a favor and read this book. It could enhance your life, both physically and emotionally, and possibly add years to your life span. Surveys show that many teens say they are overweight. They are eager to shed pounds, but have been largely unsuccessful in their efforts. This well documented and clearly written book provides solid advice on healthy ways to reach and maintain one's ideal weight. Vital topics, such as self-esteem, diets, exercise, and nutrition, are addressed.

At a time when obesity is considered the number one health threat to teenagers, this book offers a fresh message of hope.

Chapter One

The United States has become one of the world's fattest nations. According to recent studies, about one-third of American children and adolescents are obese or overweight.

Dire Health Warning

According to health and government experts, being too fat has become a world-wide epidemic. A 2011 report in the presti- medical journal Lancet found that obesity is a greater threat to global health than is ger. The United States may not be the fattest ion on the planet, but it ranks in the top 10, cording to data from the World Health rganization (WHO). Nearly two out of three mericans are overweight or obese, and obesity anks among the leading causes of preventable death in the United States, reports the U.S. Centers for Disease Control and Prevention (CDC). It's estimated that about 300,000 Americans die each year as a result of obesity-related conditions.

Many overweight Americans are teenagers. More than 17 percent of Americans age 12 to 19 are overweight, meaning they are 20 or more pounds above the normal weight for their height. Among the same age group, about 18 percent are considered obese, or severely overweight—30 or more pounds above normal for their height with a body mass index (BMI) of over 30 (BMI is a useful indicator of excess weight that uses height and weight in its calculation).

"[Obesity is] the public health issue of our generation. We right now are assigning our kids to a decreased quality of life," says Dr. James Hill, a nutrition expert at the University of Colorado. "They're going to have chronic diseases. They're going to be on multiple drugs at age 20. This is totally unacceptable [to] doom our kids to all the consequences of being obese."

If the obesity trend continues, many of today's teenagers may not live past middle age. One study that tracked 128,000 Norwegians over the past 40 years found that people who were obese as teens have an average life expectancy of 46 years—33 years shorter than the overall average life expectancy in Norway.

Scientists in the United States and elsewhere have seen a troubling new trend of weight-related diseases emerging in teens. Young people are now affected by heart disease, type II diabetes, arthritis, high blood pressure, arteriosclerosis, liver disease, and a host of other chronic ailments once common only among older adults. A June 2004 study in the *New England Journal of Medicine* warned that "a dramatic increase in the incidence of type II diabetes may represent only the tip of the iceberg and may herald the emergence of an epidemic of advanced cardiovascular disease" as teens become young adults.

Why So Much Obesity and Why Now?

Many of today's teens were raised on truly bad diets, nurtured by prepackaged foods high in calories and fat. The consumption of sodas, highly sugared fruit drinks, and high-calorie sports drinks has increased the daily caloric intake of today's teens by an average of nearly 300 calories above the 2,000-calorie total needed for most females or the 2,500-calorie total required for most males. Those 300 soda calories alone, according to experts, are enough to cause steady weight gain.

In addition, American teens today are burning fewer calories than teens of previous generations. They are sitting around more than ever before, their attention captured by television, video games, and other electronic diversions. Social scientists have found that these pursuits not only keep teens inactive, but also create a feeding environment—an enticement to eat and drink during the hours in front of the TV or the computer.

Schools provide little help in the fight against fat. Tight budgets have caused schools all over the United States to cut back on gym classes and eliminate athletic teams. Much of the food served in school cafeterias is not particularly nutritious. According to the Gallup Youth Survey, two out of three teens can purchase soda and candy in vending machines at their schools.

The evolving nature of families in the United States has contributed to the decline in good nutrition. There are many more single-parent homes today than there were a generation ago; in many homes of two-parent families, both parents must work to make ends meet. As a result, meals prepared at home for the entire family have often been replaced by take-out and fast-food meals. Although greater reliance on commercially prepared meals means less time in the kitchen for busy parents, it also means their families are eating fewer fresh vegetables and fruits while consuming more food high in calories, fats, and processed sugars.

Scientific study of obesity has so far painted a discouraging pic-

A high school student makes a purchase from a vending machine in his school. The ready availability of processed snack foods high in fat and calories is a major contributor to the problem of obesity.

ture. Experts have found that genes play a big part in controlling hunger, metabolism, and the ways in which the body burns energy. These genes tell the body how to regulate fat, a complicated process related to human survival. Throughout most of human history, people have had to store fat to survive famines, wars, and other emergencies. In modern life, these deeply rooted survival traits motivate people to eat too much. Cravings that once saved lives during times of hardship now make people fat in times of plenty.

On the other side of the obesity crisis are the teenagers who obsess about being thin because they are so afraid of being fat. One 1999 study found that 44 percent of 14-year-old girls were trying to lose weight. Eating disorders are on the rise. One in three dieters engages in unhealthy weight-loss practices, and one in five teens develops an eating disorder. Anorexia nervosa, a dangerous plunge into starvation that once only affected a small percentage of white females, is now showing up in guys and is a leading cause of death among teenage girls.

This book explores these issues in detail, looking at the latest research. Results from the Gallup Youth Survey, along with professional analysis and firsthand accounts by adolescents, reveal truths about teens' diets, their bodies, and their habits. There are a number of key questions related to this issue. What causes teens to gain weight at a pace never before seen? How does the body store and burn fat, and why are young people especially vulnerable to weight problems? What social and family changes make weight gain more likely to occur? Why do many diets fail? How does dieting turn into a disease for some teens? What are the physical effects of obesity and its associated diseases, and how are they diagnosed? Finally, how can teens combat overweight and obesity and turn the tide against their greatest health threat?

Chapter Two

In recent years scientists have found that a person's weight is determined by more than just what he or she eats. There is a genetic component to metabolism that contributes to a person's body type and weight.

The Science of Weight and Metabolism

When people eat, their bodies convert food to energy through a process known as metabolism. This process, in conjunction with the factors of diet and exercise, helps determine body weight. Metabolism is sometimes described as the body's furnace, in which food is burned as fuel to create energy. Even when people are not active — resting or asleep, for example — their metabolism is working to burn energy to sustain their basic biological functions, such as breathing, heartbeat, and brain activity. These basic functions use most of our energy — up to 65 percent of daily energy use, according to scientists Michael Goran and Margarita Treuth.

In the discussion of weight and nutrition issues, food is generally measured as potential energy, and the standard measure of energy contained in food is the calorie. In scientific terms, a calorie is the amount of energy it takes to raise a gram of water by 1° Celsius.

Food can be classified into three basic substances: carbohydrates, proteins, and fats. Each has special functions essential to human survival. When a person eats carbohydrates—which are found in bread, potatoes, apples, and starchy foods—the body quickly converts them to glucose, a basic sugar the body uses for immediate energy. Extra carbohydrates can be stored by the body for future use as energy, but this storage process itself burns energy; if a person overeats carbohydrates, the body burns up to 20 percent of the extra carbohydrates to convert the rest into body fat.

Fats are an important part of a healthy diet: they help the body store vitamins, are necessary for healthy skin, and help the brain and other internal organs to function correctly. Food fat of the kind found in red meats and dairy products can be used by the body as energy, although it is harder for the body to burn than carbohydrates. However, it is much easier to store, requiring only 3 percent of its calories to convert into stored body fat.

The body prefers to use carbohydrates for energy whenever it can. If the body's energy needs are met from the carbohydrates eaten during a meal, any fat in the meal will be stored. A bag of potato chips, for example, is made up mostly of carbohydrates and fat. A teenager who devours too many chips will use the carbohydrates for energy needs, and if his or her resting metabolism and activity don't burn off the carbohydrates before the next feeding, the fat will be stored.

Proteins, found in meats, nuts, eggs, and some vegetables, are essential for building tissue and organs, but proteins are not burned for energy unless a person is starving and has used up all of his or her existing carbohydrates and stores of fat. This is the enticement of high-protein diets, like the Atkins program that became so popular in the late 1990s: dieters fill their stomachs with proteins that

Carbohydrates, proteins, and fats are all required for the body to function properly. Weight problems develop, however, when these substances are not eaten in the proper balance.

Physical activity helps increase a person's metabolism, the rate at which they burn calories. Teens who exercise regularly are less likely to develop weight problems.

won't be used for making fat. Their bodies burn carbohydrates and then their own body fat before burning the proteins for energy.

One interesting component of metabolism is the energy required in the activity of eating—10 percent of total caloric intake. Called the thermic effect, it is the energy consumed in eating and digesting food, and it produces detectable heat after consuming a large meal.

Some obese people tend to produce thermic heat less efficiently, thus burning fewer calories than normal while eating and digesting. Scientists believe this may reflect inefficient insulin secretion, or what is called "insulin resistance"—a major symptom of type II diabetes. Insulin is a hormone produced by the pancreas that allows muscle cells to burn glucose. If not enough insulin is produced, carbohydrates can't be burned and fat cells are more likely to build up in the blood. Unused glucose that habitually accumulates in the blood contributes to damage to the heart, eyes, kidneys, nervous system, and circulatory system.

An important part of metabolism is the burning of energy during activity, and it varies greatly with a person's movement, daily exertions, and physical routines. For example, people who twitch, wiggle, and seem never to stop moving have a great advantage in the calorie wars—fidgeting can increase a person's total daily energy use by as much as one-third. In *The Hungry Gene*, author Ellen Shell describes a recent study involving volunteers who ate 1,000 excess calories a day for two months. The participants in the study gained an average of 10 pounds, but there was a wide variation in weight gain—some only gained 2 pounds, while one gained 16. The difference was attributed almost entirely to different levels of nervous energy among the participants.

Voluntary exercise is the most easily altered component of metabolism, as it is the only component except food intake that is

CURRENT AND IDEAL WEIGHT OF YOUNG ADULTS

In a November 2002 survey, the Gallup Organization asked respondents to give their current weight, as well as what they felt was their ideal body weight. Comparing the results of the two questions gives a sense of how Americans' current weights compare with their ideal weights.

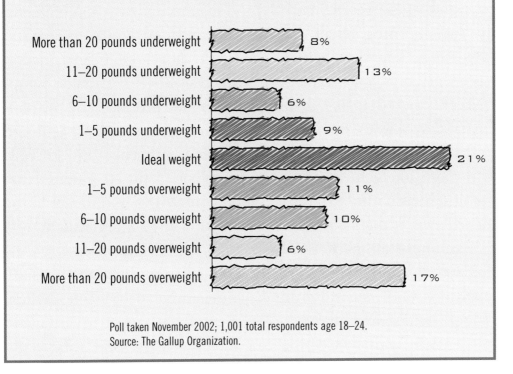

More than 20 pounds underweight — 8%
11–20 pounds underweight — 13%
6–10 pounds underweight — 6%
1–5 pounds underweight — 9%
Ideal weight — 21%
1–5 pounds overweight — 11%
6–10 pounds overweight — 10%
11–20 pounds overweight — 6%
More than 20 pounds overweight — 17%

Poll taken November 2002; 1,001 total respondents age 18–24.
Source: The Gallup Organization.

subject to dramatic change. According to Harvard physician Robert Lustig, voluntary activity may burn 5 to 50 percent of a person's total caloric intake, depending upon the person and the activities. Exercise not only burns carbohydrates and fat, but also increases insulin production and thus helps the body to burn calories more efficiently. Exercise can also increase muscle mass, which in turn increases a person's resting metabolism because the body burns additional calories to maintain muscles.

The Genetic Component of Weight

While teen overweight and obesity is partly the result of dietary decisions and physical activity, inherited genes also play a role in determining body weight by telling the body how to operate. According to scientists Nancy and Craig Warden, weight control begins with a genetically programmed fixed weight, a "body weight or fat mass 'set point'" that keeps weight surprisingly stable. The set point establishes a rate of metabolism that regulates the way in which a person's body burns calories.

Dr. Rudolph Leibel, an obesity expert at Columbia Presbyterian Medical Center in New York, says that people's bodies and minds regulate weight with remarkable consistency. In one study, when volunteers overate so that their weight should have increased by 10 percent, doctors found that their metabolisms increased by 15 percent, compensating for the extra calories. "It was as though their bodies were trying to drive their weight back down," explained reporter Gina Kolata in a *New York Times* article published on October 17, 2000. Their bodies knew what their natural weight should be, and when the volunteers lost weight by at least 10 percent, their metabolisms slowed by 15 percent. Dieting is almost always accompanied by a reduction in metabolism, and that means fewer calories are burned during activity and at rest. This is why upwards of 95 percent of people who diet soon gain all their weight back. Their bodies slow down so their fat stores can catch up.

The rate of metabolism, like other functions of body weight, is largely controlled by inherited genes, which determine how a person experiences hunger, fullness, fat storage, cravings, and even tastes for certain kinds of food. Does this mean teens are fated to have the same metabolisms as their parents? No, but it does mean they probably share many similar tendencies for handling hunger, eating, and processing food into energy.

So weight gain is not just a matter of eating too much or not being active enough. According to the Warden study, which looked at the "set points" of metabolism, there are seven identifiable genes in humans that cause obesity. The most important genes affecting obesity also regulate appetite. These highly complex genes have many pathways and back-up systems to protect people from famine, malnutrition, and starvation. Hunger can induce superhuman cravings and extraordinary motivation for survival. Turning off hunger, scientists have discovered, is very difficult because it is a powerful tool of evolution and survival.

In many ancient cultures that were confronted by famine and starvation, storing excess fat was essential to survival. A typical diet included rough, unprocessed grains and meat requiring much energy to gather and to digest. People who were not good at storing fat simply died or at least were susceptible to malnutrition, infant mortality, and reduced fertility. People who stored fat efficiently survived starvation and famine, passing their robust fat genes to their children.

Scientists believe the physical demands and hardships of ancient life prevented most people from getting fat. However, in today's era, in which food is abundant in most parts of the developed world and physical tasks are generally less strenuous, people's fat genes are working too hard for their own good. These genes, which operate mostly in the same manner as they did 100,000 years ago, have not yet adapted to today's diet and sedentary lifestyle.

Researchers have identified a key component in regulating fat called leptin. This hormone is released into the bloodstream by fat tissue as it gains mass. Leptin tells the brain to decrease appetite and increase energy consumption. Governed by genes, leptin production varies among people, and scientists have found that many obese people have leptin deficiencies. Some of the problem may be genetic and some may result from a blunting of leptin signals resulting from prolonged excessive eating. In any case, obese people with leptin malfunctions feel hungrier than they should.

Today, most young people spend much of their spare time in front of computers or television sets, rather than exercising. This sedentary lifestyle has contributed to the rising rate of obesity.

Instead of telling the brain the body should no longer be hungry, the malfunctioning leptin system tells the brain to keep on eating and minimize all other activity.

Unfortunately, experiments to increase leptin levels in overweight people generally have not worked very well, says Ellen Shell. She identifies more than a dozen critical components in the mind's electrical circuits that influence weight, including leptin, other chemical hormones, and brain signal systems. While leptin has been proven to factor importantly in the level of hunger an individual feels, adding leptin only helps those who have an apparent genetic deficiency of the hormone to lose weight.

Organs such as the liver and digestive tract are also involved in the complex chemistry affecting metabolism. They, too, help guide the brain's hunger impulses, thirst, energy levels, and moods. Increasingly, scientists and physicians are seeing overweight and obesity as disease processes, so complex that they exceed willpower and conscious control. Viewed in this light, obesity is a failure of body systems and faulty chemistry in which medical treatment is necessary.

The Wardens report that scientists are only beginning to pinpoint "a large and diverse collection of genes that can influence fat mass," and when they solidify their knowledge, new drug treatments will be developed, some based upon customized "molecular diagnosis" matched to each person's genes. So far, drug treatments have not worked especially well, and are quickly defeated by the kind of compensatory eating that returns most people to their body weight set point. Until new findings about genetic coding lead to the production of new anti-fat drugs, most people are stuck with their own fat set point and resting metabolism level; a leptin system that controls their hunger; and numerous genetic directives not yet understood.

Racial and Cultural Factors

Genes corresponding to race also affect the weight gain of people from different ethnic backgrounds. Black and Hispanic American adolescents have substantially higher rates of overweight and obesity than do whites, especially among girls. According to the CDC, 17 to 23 percent of Native American school children are obese, and native Hawaiian adolescents have much higher than average rates of obesity.

Many experts have concluded that the difference in weight among the races is the product of differing metabolisms. According to Jennifer Z. Dounchis and her team of researchers, studies indicate that "Black women and girls have been shown to have lower resting energy expenditures than white girls." Overweight minorities may struggle with adjusting to the diet of a new country. For example, although Hawaiians who consume foods high in dietary fat are more likely to be obese than whites, they generally do not have the same weight issues when they consume the traditional foods of their native diet.

A May 2004 study by the Public Policy Institute of California found that immigrants of all races live significantly longer lives than their ethnic counterparts born in the United States, even though many of them experience greater poverty and hardship. The study's authors believe new immigrants eat healthier diets and have not made the transition to the fatty, fast-food diet of their ethnic counterparts who have lived longer in the United States. Some researchers believe these traits develop over time and propose that ethnic groups that have experienced extreme poverty and starvation over the centuries have adapted and evolved to store fat more efficiently.

Chapter Three

Snacks and drinks with low nutritional value are displayed as Margo Wootan, director of nutrition policy at the Center for Science in the Public Interest, speaks during a 2003 news conference on school food nutrition. In recent years school administrators have been asked to replace soda and junk food sold in schools with healthful drinks and snacks.

Unhealthy Eating Habits

As teenagers mature, they begin to break away from their parents socially and become increasingly influenced by their peers. One consequence of this shift is that they develop new eating habits that often include more snack foods high in fat and calories, more take-out and processed foods, fewer home-cooked meals or balanced meals, and more soda or sugary drinks to wash it all down. This new diet places great stress on teens' metabolism. There is an increase in fat and carbohydrates during a time when most teens are less physically active than ever.

According to pediatric scientist Dennis M. Styne, adolescence is the most crucial time in predicting lifetime obesity. The heavier an adolescent is at one age, the more obese he or she will be at a later age, he explains. And the longer an adolescent carries excess weight, the greater the likelihood of being obese as an adult. Weight may depend in part on whether one or both parents are obese. "A toddler with no obese parents is far more likely to avoid adulthood obesity than is a child with one or two obese parents," writes Styne.

Between the ages of five and seven, children who are genetically inclined to have weight problems begin to gain excessive fat. If these children remain overweight or obese into adolescence, they are very likely to face a lifelong struggle with their weight. The health consequences of teen obesity appear to be much more dangerous than obesity that begins later in adulthood.

When young people reach puberty, they undergo rapid growth and extensive physical changes. Puberty unleashes a stampede of hormones causing new cravings and hunger to fuel the body's rapid growth. These physical changes are accompanied by emotional turmoil that disrupts inhibitions and self-regulation. Scientists believe all of this chaotic brain activity makes teens more susceptible to depression, anxiety, and mood disorders that lead to damaging behaviors centered around food and diet.

During puberty adolescents also undergo a major growth spurt. As the body's way of preparing them for motherhood, girls add fat cells that are mostly concentrated in the pelvis, buttocks, thighs, and breasts. Boys, meanwhile, tend to grow upward with a broadening of the shoulders and increased muscle mass. However, they can also accumulate fat deposits in their belly, where their excessive weight exceeds the girth of their hips. This stomach fat is a dangerous fat for males that can lead to type II diabetes, heart disease, high blood pressure, and premature death.

Unhealthy Choices

A nutritious diet is the result of proper decisions. Choosing to get a certain amount of sleep, for example, has a great impact on a diet. Because only 15 percent of teens sleep the required 8.5 hours or more on school nights, the vast majority of them skip breakfast in order to catch up on their sleep, according to the American Academy of Pediatrics (AAP). By lunchtime—perhaps 14 hours after the last meal—these teens are famished, their brains in need of calories to operate properly. Subsequently, many teens overeat at lunch, and they continue eating over the next nine hours. During this period most teens will eat at least four or five times, according to a study by the education-based Channel One Network.

In addition to missing a balanced breakfast, teens are eating a lunch largely composed of fast food. A 2003 study in the *American Journal of Public Health* reported that 90 percent of schools offer meal programs in which the students choose what they want. The study found that fried potatoes are a daily offering in most schools, and are usually chosen instead of healthy fruits and vegetables.

Students line up to receive food at the lunch counter in their school. The most popular foods served in school cafeterias, such as pizza, fried chicken strips, and french fries, are high in fat, calories, and cholesterol.

Pizza, cheeseburgers, and other foods high in calories and fat are also popular choices on school lunch menus.

Perhaps even worse is the sugary soda that teens choose to wash down their meals. A 20-ounce cup of soda, for example, contains the equivalent of 15 tablespoons of sugar—20 percent more than the recommended daily allowance of sugar. Sports drinks such as Gatorade and Powerade contain nearly as many calories. Studies have found that 75 percent of teens consume soft drinks every day, and increased soda intake is largely responsible for a 22 percent increase in sugar calories by teens since 1962. According to Kelly Brownell, author of *Food Fight*, sweetened drinks account for half the caloric intake of the average teen. However, this does not cause teens to reduce what they eat at meals—despite the extra calories, soda does not make them full, nor does it fulfill any of the body's basic nutritional needs.

Soda and soft drinks are easily available to students in their schools. Three-fourths of U.S. high schools provide soda and vending machines, and nearly half have snack bars where students can buy soda, candy, or other treats. Nearly three out of four boys and two out of three girls say they purchase candy or soda from school vending machines. In Denver, where 38 percent of teens are overweight or obese, the city's 72,000-student school district provides 10 soda machines at every high school. It is difficult for the school districts simply to get rid of the soda machines because they are a large source of revenue. For example, the *Rocky Mountain News* reported that the Denver school system expected its vending machines to bring in $8 to $12 million over a five-year period.

However, in recent years a few school districts have resisted the tempting offers of soda distributors. Philadelphia walked away from a $43-million contract with Coca-Cola, and several states, including Colorado and Maryland, are considering laws to reduce the availability of soda in schools. Other schools now require vending machines to include water and pure fruit juices as alternatives to sugared sodas. But sugar is still winning, reported Brownell in *Food Fight*. In a survey of vending machines at 10 high schools, he found that nearly 90 percent of the available choices were for sugared drinks.

High-Calorie Fast-food Meals

Most teens say that they eat junk food or fast food each week. In a 2003 poll by the Gallup Youth Survey, 23 percent confessed to eating "a great deal" of junk food. Only 2 percent said they do not eat junk food, and only 15 percent said they ate hardly any. In its

Megan McGreevy of the Philadelphia Food Trust holds up a jar containing the amount of sugar a child could consume in soft drinks during a school week. Some schools, including those in the Philadelphia School District, have removed soda vending machines because of nutritional concerns.

How would you describe your diet?

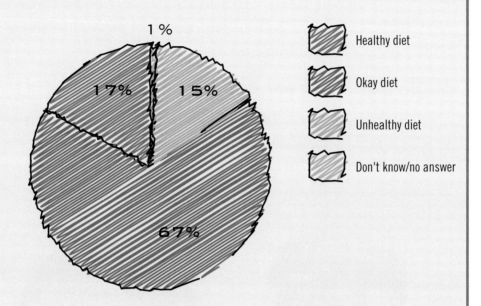

1 %

17%

15%

67%

Healthy diet

Okay diet

Unhealthy diet

Don't know/no answer

How important would you say a healthful diet is to your good health overall?

	All Teens	Boys	Girls
Very important	62%	53%	71%
Somewhat important	34%	40%	28%
Not too important	4%	6%	2%
Not important at all	1%	1%	n/a

Percentages may add up to more than 100% due to rounding.
Poll taken April–July 1998; 503 total respondents age 13–17.
Source: Gallup Youth Survey/The Gallup Organization

study of teen nutrition, the Channel One Network found that teens typically visit fast-food restaurants more than twice a week.

What are the consequences for teens who make fast food a part of their diet? First, the higher calories and fat in fast food leads to weight gain. According to diet expert Anne Collins, a 17-year-old male who is five feet ten and weighs 150 pounds needs 2,439 calories per day to maintain his weight. A 17-year-old female who is five feet three and 125 pounds requires 1,937 calories per day. An examination of typical fast-food meals shows that teens are getting far more calories than their bodies need. For example, the Fast Food Nutrition Fact Explorer, a calorie counter designed by FatCalories.com, says that a McDonald's Double Quarter-Pounder has 770 total calories and 47 grams of fat, more than 70 percent of the 65 grams recommended as a full day's quota for a 2,000-calorie daily diet. The burger's 20 grams of saturated fat exceeds the daily recommended allowance, and the sodium (salt) level of 1,440 milligrams is more than half the recommended daily allowance of 2,400 mg. Cholesterol from the double burger is 165 mg, more than half the 300-mg daily maximum.

Other fast foods are even worse. A Double Whopper at Burger King has 1,070 calories, 27 grams of saturated fat, 185 mg of cholesterol, and 1,500 mg of sodium. A 12-inch Double Meatball Sub from Subway lumbers in at 1,560 calories — nearly the whole day's caloric needs for a 17-year-old girl weighing 125 pounds, and almost two day's worth of saturated fat. A 14-inch Domino's pizza weighs in at 774 calories, and includes nearly a whole day's fat and sodium.

These figures don't include the soda and fries that come with the meals. Add 250 more calories for a 20-ounce cup of soda. Add about 500 more calories for fries, and one of these meals pretty much breaks the day's calorie limit for a teenager who is almost

The health effects of fast-food meals are apparent in the rising numbers of children and adults being treated for obesity. This "super-sized" meal may contain more calories than a young person needs for the entire day, but does not fulfill the body's nutritional requirements.

certain to eat three or four more times that day.

Writing for *HealthWatch,* Dr. Kim Mulvihill notes that studies show teens who never eat in fast-food restaurants average only 1,952 calories a day. Teens who eat fast food one to two times a week average 2,193 calories a day, and teens who eat fast food three or more times devour 2,752 calories a day—800 more calories per day than those who abstain from fast food. These surplus calories add up to increased weight for teens, especially for those not exercising to burn off the calories. As Mulvihill notes, "Eating just an extra ten calories a day adds up to an extra pound each year."

The calorie surplus is not the only problem when it comes to teenagers' diets. A study of teenage girls in the Midwest published in the journal *Adolescence* found that although many were eating more calories than they needed, their typical daily diet failed to meet many of their nutritional needs. As many as a third were of "marginal health status," reported *Adolescence.* Teenagers' bodies are still developing, and they need higher levels of protein, vitamins, iron, calcium, and other substances than adults require. Numerous studies have found that adolescent diets fall significantly short in iron, vitamin C, and protein. A recent study sponsored by the American Cancer Institute found that "unhealthy dietary

AN EXPERIMENT TURNS DANGEROUS

Independent filmmaker Morgan Spurlock decided to test the theory that eating too much fast food was unhealthy. For 30 days he ate nothing but McDonald's meals while filming a documentary, *Super Size Me,* to record his experience. Within a few days he began putting on weight, nearly a pound a day. During the filming Spurlock was followed closely by three physicians and a nutritionist, who tested him for changes in his liver, blood cholesterol, blood pressure, blood sugar, and other vital health signs. By the 21st day, his doctors were urging Spurlock to stop making the movie because his liver was showing signs of failure. His doctor told him, "You're frying your liver," exhibiting the properties of an advanced alcoholic on a fatal drinking binge.

Spurlock kept eating. When the 30 days was over, he had gained over 24 pounds, a 13 percent increase in his body weight. He suffered bouts of depression, fatigue, chest pains, sexual dysfunction, and signs of food addiction. Although he had started the experiment in excellent health, by the end of the month he had elevated cholesterol (a 65-point gain), high blood pressure, and blood sugar levels that put him at risk for a heart attack or stroke. What began as a humorous send-up of the fast-food industry turned into a risky gamble with his own health.

patterns, especially diets low in fruits and vegetables and high in fats" are linked to chronic disease in teens.

Some fast-food restaurants have been paying attention to the unhealthy effects of their meals. In March 2004, McDonald's announced that it would withdraw from the race of offering customers the largest meal. It would eliminate its "Super Size" meals, thus reducing the calories in the average meal at its franchises. However, while McDonald's has taken action regarding this issue, serving size remains a huge problem. In the United States, where serving sizes are 25 percent larger than in France, large portions sell meals and please customers.

Studies have found that the larger the meal people are served, the more they eat—regardless of whether they eat at a fast-food restaurant or at home. Brownell reports that in a study at Penn State University, subjects were fed 12-inch subs instead of the usual 8-inch. The women who participated increased their caloric intake by 11 percent and the men by 20 percent, yet they did not report any difference in how full they felt after they ate the larger meal. In another study, researchers provided macaroni and cheese lunches once a week, and over four weeks gradually increased the portions. The first week the serving size was 500 grams; by the fourth week it had become 1,000 grams. People ate 30 percent more when given the largest serving size. In another study with potato chips, women given a six-ounce bag instead of a three-ounce bag ate 18 percent more chips, while men ate 35 percent more. According to Brownell, most Americans eat like the subjects of these studies because they do not have an accurate estimate of serving size or of calories. They also underestimate their daily caloric intake by about 25 percent.

Family Patterns and Healthy Eating

While fast-food restaurants help shape the nation's poor diet, they cannot be completely blamed for the fat epidemic. Eating habits begin at home, and experts believe that family behaviors contribute to the problem. According to Penn State University researchers Leann Birch and Kirsten Davison, parents with a genetic propensity for being overweight "are likely to select environments for themselves and their children, including low levels of activity and high fat intake" that cause weight gain. Parents have eating styles—ranging from high tolerance for fats to strict control over portion sizes—that they impose on their children, or which children absorb by example. They not only supply food, but pressure their children to eat certain foods and dictate how frequently they eat. Parents who are obese often enjoy fatty,

Parents have the power to help shape their children's eating habits by serving home-cooked meals regularly and encouraging healthy eating habits.

starchy foods and offer them to their children. They are also less likely to engage in physical activity alone or with their children.

Parents thus provide not only the genetic blueprint for eating, but they are also the primary role models for eating preferences and behavior. A key factor in developing food preferences in children is introducing new foods. According to Birch and Davison, most people and especially children resist new foods, especially healthy ones. "People's genetic predisposition to prefer sweet and salty foods means those foods will be accepted readily," they explain. But the more healthful meats, vegetables, fruits, and fibers require more extensive experience before they are accepted. Both parents and children need to work harder at learning to like healthy food.

However, parents must use caution in putting too much pressure on their children to eat healthy food, because striving to control children's eating habits may backfire. If parents are too strict, their children never learn self-control, which is the key to healthy eating. Birch and Davison argue that parental pressure is often counterproductive. "Rather than fostering food acceptance," they write, "pressuring and coercing children to eat particular foods promotes dislike of those foods."

Another common but problematic parental practice is forcing children to completely finish their meals even when they say that they are full. A child forced to do this "may learn to ignore her internal feedback signaling feelings of fullness," write Birch and Davison. That important check on eating too much may later fail in the teen years when eating is often unaccompanied by parents. Similarly, children who say they are hungry and are told to wait until mealtime "may learn it is the presence of food, not hunger, that should initiate eating." When parents blunt natural eating instincts such as hunger and fullness, children may lose touch with appetite signals from the brain that are essential to moderate eating. Aggressive parental coaching can lead to "chronic dieting . . . binge eating, problems of energy balance and overweight."

If close supervision does not work, what is the solution to fostering good eating habits? Birch and Davison say that it has been observed in studies that children given a variety of healthy foods without parental coercion selected "diets that supported adequate growth and health. The secret to the children's success was the array of healthy, unseasoned, unprocessed foods that were offered."

Yet another mistake is giving children portions that are too large. Studies show that children as young as five begin to eat more when given larger portions, so parents who provide large helpings will actually build larger appetites in their children even if the calories are not needed.

In addition to overcoming these genetic and behavioral factors, teenagers would be better served if they ate more home-cooked food. A 2004 Gallup Youth Survey found that a quarter of families ate together at home three or fewer days a week and only 28 percent ate together at home seven days a week. By contrast, 40 percent of Canadian families and 38 percent of families in the United Kingdom ate dinner together each night. During the 1960s, when most households included only one working parent outside the home, homemakers spent on average two and a half hours making dinner, according to Shell. By 1996 that cooking time had shrunk to only 15 minutes, with much of the labor replaced by frozen or microwavable dinners heavily laced with fats, starches, sugars, and salt.

Experts argue that the changing structure of the household over the decades has strongly affected the family meal. A January 2004 Gallup report found that nearly four out of five women with school-age children worked outside the home and that the number of single-parent households had tripled since 1970 to 31 percent of all American families. In a 2003 Gallup Youth Survey, pollsters found that 20 percent of teens ate "fast food either 'every day' or 'several times a week.'" Nearly half of every dollar spent on food in the United States is for restaurant meals, according to the National Restaurant Association, and a 2004 NPD FoodWorld survey reported that three out of four restaurant visits were made to fast-food establishments.

Hanging Out

When school is over, most teens are largely sedentary. A third of them like to hang out with friends or family, nearly 24 percent watch TV, and nearly 30 percent use a computer five or more hours a week, according to recent Gallup data. Boys are more avid TV watchers than girls: more than a quarter of male teens watch 10 to 20 hours of TV a week, and 14 percent watch 20 or more hours a week. One in three girls watches 5 to 10 hours a week, 17 percent watch 10 to 20 hours, and 8 percent watch more than 20 hours. The Gallup Youth Survey indicated an interesting connection between diet and TV watching. "Thirty-seven percent of teens who say they eat a poor diet watch 10 or more hours of television a week," the survey noted, "compared with 23 percent of teens who say they eat a healthy diet."

Several studies show that television contributes to overweight and obesity by providing, in the words of Lori Francis, "a context for eating." Francis and her research colleagues at Penn State University found that TV viewing directly influenced weight gain among young girls ages five to nine whose parents were not overweight—proof that environment, not genetic factors, was likely at

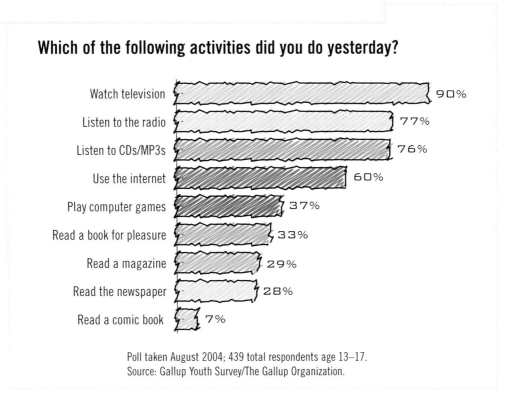

Which of the following activities did you do yesterday?

Watch television	90%
Listen to the radio	77%
Listen to CDs/MP3s	76%
Use the internet	60%
Play computer games	37%
Read a book for pleasure	33%
Read a magazine	29%
Read the newspaper	28%
Read a comic book	7%

Poll taken August 2004; 439 total respondents age 13–17.
Source: Gallup Youth Survey/The Gallup Organization.

play. Internet use provides a similar context for snacking.

Television advertising is also partly responsible for children eating fewer vegetables and fruits, according to an article published in the journal *Pediatrics* in 2003. Over half the 20,000 ads viewed by children each year involve food, and nearly half of these include fatty and sugary foods. Many of these ads claim that these foods are "nutritious or healthy." The *Pediatrics* study reported that nearly all breakfast cereal ads "asserted that the food was part of a 'balanced' or 'complete' breakfast." Advertising may foster misconceptions about nutrition that contradict national dietary standards, wrote the authors, who noted that in 1992 the American Academy of Pediatrics "recommended the eradication of televised food advertising toward children." Nutritionists have observed that many

In addition to being convenient, fast food is less expensive than healthful food such as fresh fruit and vegetables. As a result, the rate of obesity and malnutrition among America's poor is increasing.

children pay close attention to commercials for food products. A study conducted in Liverpool, England, found that obese children have much better recall of food advertisements than lean children. In both groups all the children ate more after watching food ads.

Perhaps the most important effect of television watching, however, is that it "reduces resting metabolism," according to Stanford University professor Dr. Thomas Robinson. Watching television is a passive and relaxing activity, and it seems to cool the fat furnace that burns calories even while the body is not active. Internet use produces similar results. In 2011, according to the media research firm Nielsen, American teens spent on average 11.5 hours per month online. That was in addition to more than seven hours per month teens with smartphones spent watching video on their mobile devices.

Economic Factors

The fat-saturated and unhealthy diet linked to worldwide obesity is also cheaper and much more convenient than the healthy diet, writes Kelly Brownell in *Food Fight*. "Healthy food is harder to get, less convenient, promoted very little, and more expensive," he argues.

Healthy food is more difficult to get in poorer, predominantly black neighborhoods. In a North Carolina study, for example, only 8 percent of African Americans lived in a neighborhood with a supermarket, whereas 31 percent of whites had their own neighborhood supermarket. In Hartford, Connecticut, the number of urban supermarket chains dropped from 13 in 1968 to just 2 in 2013. In low-income areas of Los Angeles, there is one supermarket for every 28,000 people. Because people suffer from a lack of shopping options, they are presented with food that is generally cheaper in quality and less healthful. Small "mom and pop" markets and convenience stores, which are much more common in inner cities than supermarkets, seldom offer fresh vegetables and rely heavily on frozen and packaged foods. The prices are also higher in convenience stores than in supermarkets, making fast-food meals seem relatively inexpensive. In addition, it is harder for poorer people, who are less likely to have cars, to travel outside of their neighborhoods to shop for food.

Fast-food restaurants are more commonly found in poorer neighborhoods than in affluent ones. For working parents too busy to cook and shop, fast food is often the only alternative for feeding a family. As a result, reports Brownell, "Obesity is now a greater threat to the health and well-being of America's poor" than hunger.

Chapter Four

Family and friends of Christy Henrich stand by the flower-adorned coffin at her funeral. Henrich, one of the best gymnasts in the United States in the late 1980s, developed the eating disorder anorexia nervosa because she believed she needed to be thinner to be competitive. She was 5-foot-3 and weighed 61 pounds when she died in 1994.

Health Consequences of Overweight and Obesity

Diseases and conditions related to weight gain divide themselves into three clusters. Each of these has a physical dimension, a psychological dimension, or a combination of both. One major cluster includes diseases either directly caused by or associated with obesity. Many of these are chronic or progressive illnesses, such as type II diabetes and heart disease, that begin during adolescence but are usually not life-threatening until adulthood. The great concern about the rapid growth in teen obesity is that these chronic diseases will become fatal more quickly because they are now starting earlier.

The second major cluster of conditions includes disorders that derive from a fear of fat. Among these are anorexia nervosa, bulimia, and binge eating disorder, each of which can lead to serious health problems. Advanced cases of anorexia can lead to death.

The third major cluster, which can overlap the other two described above, includes emotional disorders such as depression and anxiety. Sometimes these disorders trigger the other eating conditions; other times the disorders result from the conditions. Often the individual faces a complex mixture of disorders and conditions, each feeding on the other to make matters worse.

Type II Diabetes, Pre-diabetes, and Metabolic Disorder

According to the American Diabetes Association (ADA), more than 15 million people suffer from type II diabetes, a serious and progressive insulin disorder that can lead to blindness, heart attacks, strokes, kidney failure, amputations of feet or legs, clinical depression, and death. Type II diabetes used to be called adult-onset diabetes until only a few years ago because it seldom struck before middle age. But now it is found in so many young people that the old name has been discarded.

Although national statistics are incomplete, the available information on the rising rates of diabetes is alarming. The city of Cincinnati, for example, began tracking the frequency of type II diagnoses in 1982. At that time, there were 0.7 cases per 100,000 kids ages 10 to 19. By 1994, the rate among young people had risen to 7.2 cases per 100,000, a tenfold jump. Each year between 2002 and 2005, according to the CDC, some 3,600 Americans under the age of 20 were newly diagnosed with type II diabetes. But because the disease is difficult to diagnose in children, the actual number of new cases was probably significantly higher.

Alarmed by the national increase in cases of type II diabetes, the ADA launched a conference in 1999 to explore the emerging problem. It discovered that 85 percent of type II diabetic youths were either overweight or obese and were most frequently diagnosed between the ages of 12 and 16. At least three out of four teens who were diagnosed had parents or close relatives with type II diabetes, thus suggesting a strong genetic link.

The ADA conference experts noted that the increase in growth hormones during adolescence sometimes causes a decline in the effectiveness of insulin. This means that glucose, the crucial blood sugars that fuel muscles, cannot be absorbed into the muscles properly. Hence, the muscles can't burn the glucose fast enough, and much of it continues to circulate in the blood where it damages blood vessels.

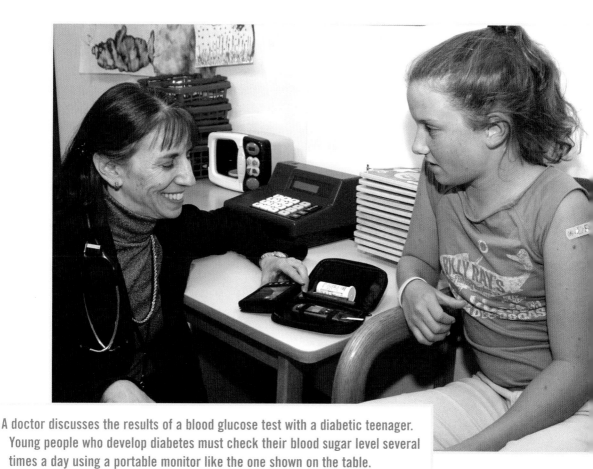

A doctor discusses the results of a blood glucose test with a diabetic teenager. Young people who develop diabetes must check their blood sugar level several times a day using a portable monitor like the one shown on the table.

According to National Institutes of Health guidelines at the National Diabetes Information Clearinghouse, diabetes has numerous symptoms. These include frequent infections that are not easily healed, frequent urination, extreme hunger or unusual thirst, blurred vision, extreme weakness, fatigue, irritability, nausea, dry and itchy skin, and loss of feeling in the hands or feet. If some of these symptoms appear, patients are encouraged to undergo a test for their blood glucose levels.

The blood test can reveal several levels of potential trouble, including pre-diabetes, which indicates a high risk for type II diabetes. Another risk factor is metabolic syndrome, a combination of medical problems diagnosed by high blood pressure, high glucose levels, unhealthy cholesterol levels, and a waist measurement that is higher than 35 inches for females and 40 inches for males. Certain minorities—such as African Americans, American Indians, Hispanic Americans, Asians, and South Pacific Islanders—are especially at risk for this condition. Teens in these ethnic groups who are overweight or have parents with type II diabetes should be tested, experts say, because if they are found to have diabetes or its precursors, they can begin treatment and halt further damage. According to a *Time* magazine article published on December 8, 2003, teens with type II diabetes "are more likely to develop heart disease in their 20s and 30s," as well as suffer from kidney disease, sexual dysfunction, eye disease, and a severely curtailed quality of life.

The encouraging news is that type II diabetes can be prevented or significantly slowed, and because insulin tends to regain its efficiency after adolescence, teens have the opportunity to prevent a progressive disease from taking root. The crucial first steps are exercise—at least 30 minutes every day—and a diet of high-fiber, low-fat foods with lots of fruits and vegetables. There are an array of medications that people can take to reduce glucose levels. Those who successfully halt type II diabetes usually lose considerable weight and keep it off through regular exercise.

High Blood Pressure, High Cholesterol, Heart Disease, and Stroke

Obesity ages the heart and blood vessels and sets in motion the diseases that kill more people than any other cause. Dennis M. Styne reported in *Pediatric Clinics of America* that 58 percent of overweight youngsters ages 5 to 17 had at least one cardiac risk factor, and in a study of autopsied males ages 15 to 19, 2 percent had advanced coronary disease of the sort experienced by elderly people. Obese children have a 10 times greater chance than normal children to have adult-level high blood pressure, says Styne, yet doctors typically don't detect these conditions, which cause few, if any, symptoms. Most people don't feel any pain until too late, but once heart disease takes its course, negative symptoms include an enlarged and weakened heart; bulges in veins, arteries, and organs called aneurysms; reduced blood circulation in the kidneys; hardened and plaque-infested arteries; and weakened blood vessel tissue that can cause blindness. The National Institutes of Health (NIH) reports that once high blood pressure develops, "it usually lasts a lifetime."

Blood pressure is most easily understood by using an example of garden hoses. To fill a garbage can, a three-quarter-inch hose carries more water than a smaller half-inch hose and can thus fill the can faster. Even though a large hose will fill the barrel more quickly, the smaller hose will squirt farther because the water is under greater pressure trying to squeeze through the smaller opening. Blood vessels follow the same principle. Ideally, the body wants the heart to deliver the most blood possible to organs and muscles, so arteries need to carry lots of blood. But if they begin to

WHAT IS BLOOD PRESSURE?

Each time the heart beats, it pumps out blood into the arteries. According to the NIH definition, "Blood pressure is the force of the blood pushing against the walls of the arteries." A blood pressure score measures two forms of pressure: systolic and diastolic. A score of 120/70* indicates normal blood pressure. The first number, 120, indicates systolic pressure—when the heart is beating and pressure is highest. The second number, 70, represents diastolic pressure—when the heart is at rest and pressure is lower. According to the NIH, a blood pressure reading of 140/90 or higher indicates high blood pressure, or hypertension. Prehypertension is a condition that, without treatment, can lead to hypertension.

Categories for Blood Pressure Levels in Adults

Category	Systolic (1st number)	Diastolic (2nd number)
Normal	Less than 120	Less than 80
Pre-hypertension	120–139	80–89
High Blood Pressure (Stage 1)	140–159	90–99
High Blood Pressure (Stage 2)	160 or higher	100 or higher

*These figures are measured in mmHg—millimeters of mercury—a standard measure also reflected in BP cuffs and machines.
Source: National Heart, Lung, and Blood Institute

become clogged and shrink to a smaller size, more pressure will be required to move the same amount of blood. In order for the smaller arteries to deliver an equal amount of blood, the heart must work harder to create more pressure. As a result of poor diet and lack of exercise, arteries become clogged with sticky plaque from high cholesterol, shrinking the opening for blood flow. The heart needs to work harder and faster to supply organs and muscles with oxygen and nutrients, and it ages prematurely under the load.

The plaque buildup from high blood cholesterol makes arteries smaller, more rigid, more prone to ruptures, and more prone to dangerous blood clots. It also damages arterial walls. Heart attacks can result either directly from clots or indirectly from weakened and damage tissue to the overworked heart. "A clot in the coronary artery interrupts the flow of blood and oxygen to the heart muscle, leading to the death of heart cells in that area," says the NIH. "The damaged heart muscle loses its ability to contract, and the remaining heart muscle needs to compensate for that weakened area." Each year, approximately 715,000 Americans suffer a heart attack, and about 125,000 die as a result.

Strokes can occur when clots travel to the brain and cause a blockage of blood flow to other parts of the brain. Or they can also occur when weakened arteries stoked by high blood pressure burst in the brain, flooding surrounding brain tissue with blood. The result in either case is brain damage or death. According to the NIH, "Stroke accounts for one out of every 15 deaths in the United States. It is the third leading cause of death in most developed countries, and the leading cause of disability in adults." Medical experts fear that heart disease and strokes will strike sooner and with more severity if the underlying conditions of overweight and obesity in teens continue to climb.

Arthritis, Sleep Apnea, Asthma, and Liver Damage

Being obese as a teenager places stress on knees, hips, and other joints and can cause premature arthritis (inflamed and painful joints). It also can cause improper alignment of hip and leg joints, producing such pain from the hip to the foot that the patient cannot walk, according to Styne. Other orthopedic problems include flat feet, bowing of the legs, and hampered bone development. These conditions are not only painful but they prevent or inhibit exercise and other activities that are necessary for maintaining proper weight and restoring good health.

Obesity in teens also causes an elevated risk of asthma. One in five obese adolescents was diagnosed with asthma in a 1999 study conducted in Mississippi, and Styne states the incidence of asthma among obese children may be close to 30 percent, which is double the estimates of asthma in normal school-age patients up to age 16. Obesity increases bronchial spasms during exercise and inhibits lung function, making exercise more difficult or impossible. Another related breathing problem is sleep apnea, which disrupts breathing during sleep. The result of a buildup of fat deposits in the breathing passages, sleep apnea can cause heart failure in extreme cases, and at the very least causes persistent snoring and frequent waking. In one obesity study, Styne reports, all obese kids snored and lost sleep. Sleep loss can in turn lead to poor school performance, chronic sleepiness, hyperactivity, and irritability.

The majority of obesity cases are caused by a poor diet, which can cause an increase in liver enzymes that damage the liver. Liver damage can manifest itself in a form of hepatitis sometimes found in alcoholics. It may progress to cirrhosis of the liver, a potentially fatal condition. It is especially dangerous if teenagers with this condition consume alcohol.

Weight loss and improved fitness levels can diminish or reduce the effects of all these conditions. However, these illnesses are

WHAT IS CHOLESTEROL?

According to the NIH, "Cholesterol is a waxy, fat-like substance that is found in all cells of the body." It is used to make hormones and substances that help digest foods. It is also found in vitamin D, and in fats that don't mix well with blood. To allow cholesterol to travel in the bloodstream, the body places it into small packages called lipoproteins, made of lipids (fat) on the inside and proteins on the outside. Two kinds of lipoproteins carry cholesterol: LDL cholesterol, referred to as the "bad" plaque-infested greasy kind and HDL, the "good" kind that carries greasy plaque back to the liver for cleanup and removal. Too much LDL causes plaque buildup in the arteries and too little HDL prevents artery clean-up. The result is high blood cholesterol—not enough good guys and too many bad guys.

For some time now, the medical consensus has been that high blood cholesterol is determined by a score of about 190 mg/dl (190 milligrams per deciliter of blood) or higher, but recent studies suggest that lower cholesterol levels reduce heart deaths dramatically. In a Harvard study whose results were reported in March 2004, a group of cholesterol-lowering drugs called statins were used in heavy doses to lower cholesterol to 62 mg/dl in hospitalized heart patients. The medication led to a 28 percent lower chance of dying than even those with 100 mg/dl scores, the *Boston Globe* reported. The initial success of these drugs indicates that medicine can dramatically lower the cholesterol of people with dangerously high levels, but physicians warn that the drugs alone cannot reduce obesity, type II diabetes, or other cardiac risk factors, and they may produce side effects in some patients.

chronic and will cause damage over time and reduce life expectancy. What scientists are discovering, much to their distress, is that these disease processes are more advanced in obese teens than anyone had expected.

Cancer

Insulin is crucial in preparing glucose for use by the muscles, but too much insulin, such as the kind sparked by processed flours, excess sugar, and low-fiber starches, can be harmful. Insulin is basically a growth hormone, and if secreted in excess it can stimulate cancer cell growth. Moreover, unless people exercise and burn off fat, insulin will also work to store fat, which can produce and regulate hormones that are implicated in colon and prostate cancer, diseases that kill over 250,000 people a year.

Pancreatic cancer, which is usually fatal, also potentially strikes people with insulin imbalances, afflicting diabetics more than others and sparing people who exercise. The key factor in cancer prevention is vigorous activity and exercise, which burns fat and promotes healthy insulin levels.

The Emotional Wreckage of Fat

In 2003 the *Journal of the American Medical Association (JAMA)* published a special issue about America's obesity crisis, and one study revealed an especially shocking fact: obese adolescents experience a quality of life comparable to that of adolescents diagnosed with cancer and suffering from the crippling effects of chemotherapy. According to the study, obese adolescents are more than five times more socially impaired than normal children and four times more socially handicapped in school functions.

Low quality of life often leads to depression. Researchers have conducted many studies on the relationship between depression and obesity. A 2002 study at Cincinnati Children's Hospital found that depression contributes to weight gain more than weight gain contributes to depression. According to the lead researcher, Dr.

Obese teenagers often struggle with self-esteem. This can have an adverse effect on their social lives.

TEENS' OPINIONS OF PEOPLE WHO ARE OVERWEIGHT

Teens were asked if they agree with the following:	Agree with statements
Teenagers are too worried about what they weigh	92%
You feel the same about over-weight people as you do about everyone else	83%
You notice very fat people when they walk by on the street	74%
People who are overweight or fat get too little respect	73%
You feel sorry for people who are very overweight or fat	71%
You like people who are very fat	64%
People who are thin have a better chance to be successful in life	45%
When you see a very fat person, you wonder what's going wrong in his or her life	41%
You find fat people attractive	19%
People who are very overweight or very fat disgust you	14%

Poll taken March–June 1997; 491 total respondents age 13–17. Source: The Gallup Organization.

Elizabeth Goodman, "This study provides evidence that depressed mood increases the risk of developing obesity in adolescence and of continuing to remain obese during adolescence." After a year of being depressed, the odds of becoming obese double, the study showed.

In adults major depressive disorder is defined by prolonged feelings of hopelessness, sadness, pessimism, loss of concentration, sleeplessness, and loss of sex drive. It lasts many weeks and is not necessarily a reaction to a specific event or experience. But adolescent depression is often trickier to diagnose, according to Dr. Koplewicz. It may resemble the adult form but may also be characterized by high levels of irritability; hypersensitivity; numerous stormy, negative interactions with friends and family; excessive sleep; and eating too much and too often. The symptoms are often overlooked because parents and teachers think that adolescence is naturally a stormy stage of life.

Another more mild form of depression is called dysthymic disorder or dysthymia, a low-level gloom experienced on most days for an average of four years. Adolescent depression is very often characterized by acting out, aggressive behavior, high anxiety, physical aches and pains, stomach complaints, headaches, and sudden good moods that last for a few hours before the teen will tumble back into gloom and irritability.

The question of whether obesity causes depression is less clear to scientists, but they do know that teens who are teased about their weight are two to three times more likely to attempt suicide. A 2003 study of teens published in the *Archives of Pediatrics and Adolescent Medicine* found that 30 percent of the girls and 25 percent of the boys had been teased about their weight by peers, and 29 percent of the girls and 16 percent of the boys had been teased by their families. Study author Marla Eisenberg reported to the website WebMD.com that "being teased is a profound experience for these kids." Another study of North Carolina children ages 9 to 16 found that obesity caused an increased risk for depression, according to *HealthScout News*, with boys more vulnerable than girls. The study also found that obesity contributes to "oppositional defiant disorder," a condition characterized by hostile and combative behaviors toward authority figures.

Anorexia Nervosa, Bulimia, and Extreme Dieting

Because the stigma of obesity is so great, there is an array of psychological problems—called eating disorders—that are as much a part of the teen obesity epidemic as the physical effects of being obese. Eating disorders, most of which involve a morbid fear of fat, are the flipside of the obesity issue. The most serious disease driven by fear of fat is anorexia nervosa, which afflicts up to 4 percent of females, according to the National Institutes of Mental Health. About half of 1 percent of the females in this group die each year, usually from complications related to the disorder, such as heart attacks or malnutrition, or from suicide. This death rate is "about 12 times higher than the annual death rate due to all causes of death among females ages 15 to 24," according to the NIMH. About one in ten individuals suffering from the condition is male, and the incidence rate for males is on the rise.

Anorexics develop an intensifying fear of weight gain and become obsessed with their appearance and eating habits. They frequently see themselves as being fatter than they are and often deny that they are becoming frightfully thin. They usually develop extremely fussy, even bizarre eating habits that may include weighing their food, selecting only a few things they will eat, and then eating those foods in very small quantities. As the disease progresses, patients often lose some of their hair as a result of malnutrition, and their menstrual cycles stop. Their muscles waste away, their bones and fingernails turn brittle, their stomachs revolt with excess acid which, in combination with vomiting, damages teeth. Eventually the electrolytes in the blood that control nerve signals and delivery of oxygen to the heart, kidneys, and crucial organs can become so unbalanced that the anorexic may suddenly die.

To continue to lose weight, some anorexics exercise compulsively with great intensity and frequency, says the NIMH. They

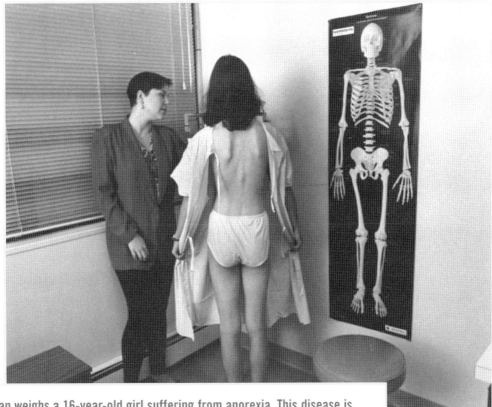

A dietician weighs a 16-year-old girl suffering from anorexia. This disease is serious and life-threatening, and requires lifelong therapy to overcome.

may also attempt to cut down their caloric intake through "purging by means of vomiting and abuse of laxatives, enemas, and diuretics." (This practice is also the main symptom of bulimia.) The anorexic's fear of gaining weight becomes a fixation, a baffling mental block against eating.

Despite the great amount of attention the scientific community has given to anorexia, experts have still not completely figured out the condition. In particular, they wonder why friends, family, therapists, and physicians have such difficulty convincing anorexics to recognize their peril and to eat. One psychologist, Dr. Shan Guisinger, has put forward a theory that anorexia is much more than a mental illness and has physiological roots that go far back into ancient history. In a 2003 story published in the *Boston Globe*, Guisinger explained that the ability to shut off hunger and engage in strenuous migrations may have provided important advantages for early survival, allowing people to carry out very hard work while on the verge of starvation or during times of war. Their brains would have been flooded with serotonin and endorphins, giving them a false immunity to pain and suffering. Female menstrual cycles might have stopped, ensuring they would not be burdened by pregnancy. Guisinger believes anorexics who fail to recognize the urgency of their starvation may be responding to these ancient signals and are simply incapable of acknowledging the dangers they face. In a similar manner to how some scientists approach obesity, Guisinger considers anorexia as a residual instinct of primitive life, a basic response to conditions seldom found in the modern era.

Experts believe that the cycle of anorexia can be set off by depression, physical illness, surgery, and other major disruptions to eating cycles. Many have concluded that some people are genetically disposed to anorectic symptoms. A majority of psychologists also fault modern culture and social pressure to be thin as triggers for anorexia. For about half the people diagnosed, the condition becomes a chronic, lifelong struggle.

Bulimia afflicts about 4 percent of the female population, and while seldom life-threatening, it is a wrenching struggle against fat. Bulimics fear gaining weight yet often engage in binge eating, stuffing themselves and then guiltily sneaking off to vomit away the excess calories. According to the NIMH, "People with bulimia often perform the behaviors in secrecy, feeling disgusted and ashamed when they binge, yet relieved once they purge." Like anorexics, they often feel repelled by their body fat and use laxatives, diuretics, enemas, or pills to prevent weight gain. They often engage in fasting and/or obsessive exercise, but usually don't cross the line into the anorectic world of starvation. For both conditions, psychiatric counseling and behavioral therapy is the only treatment. The patient often undergoes treatment for many months and even years.

Binge-Eating Disorder

A condition similar to bulimia is known as binge-eating disorder. The most significant distinction between these disorders is that binge eaters do not normally engage in a purge cycle. They eat ravenously until they are uncomfortably stuffed, and may consume large amounts even when not hungry. They often eat alone to hide their behavior, and feel guilt and disgust at themselves afterward. Binge eaters may be overweight, but they usually appear healthy. They are obsessively drawn to food and then repelled by it. Instead of purging, they are more likely to undergo cycles of intense dieting and exercise as a reaction to their guilt

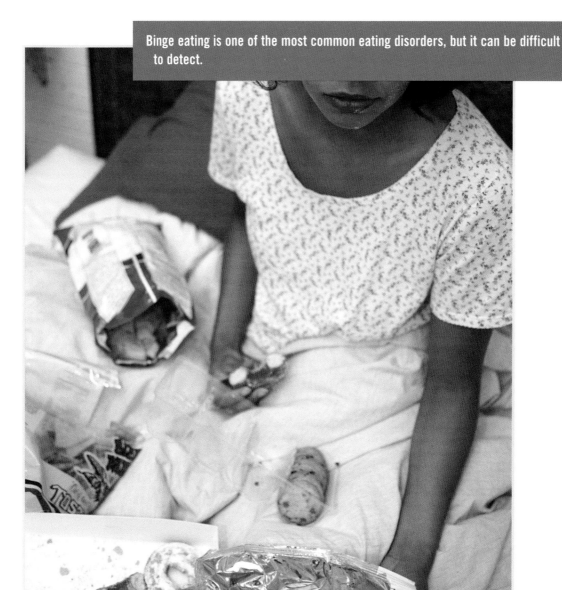

Binge eating is one of the most common eating disorders, but it can be difficult to detect.

and weight gain, according to researchers at Columbia University and the New York Psychiatric Institute.

Many other teens not diagnosed with eating disorders nonetheless engage in extreme dieting techniques. According to an August 2002 study in the *Journal of Adolescent Health*, one in three teen girls trying to lose weight engages in at least one "extreme and potentially harmful" weight-control technique such as fasting, diet pills, vomiting, or laxatives. Nearly one in five boys uses one of these techniques, and one in three teens uses cigarette smoking as a dieting tool. Thus even normal teens use dangerous weight-loss techniques familiar to anorexics and bulimics. In addition, skipping two meals daily and eating fewer than 1,200 calories a day are considered red flags for dangerous dieting that can lead to malnutrition. Early symptoms can include dizziness, ringing in the ears, stomach pain from excess acid, emotional irritability, swelling or puffiness of the face and extremities, irritated skin, menstrual irregularities, and anxiety.

Even well-publicized diets can be dangerous when taken to extremes. In 2002 a healthy 16-year-old girl collapsed in school and died of heart failure, according to a report in the *Southern Medical Journal*. The only cause physicians could find was the girl's adherence to a popular low-carbohydrate diet that can lead to irregular heart rhythms resulting from electrolyte disturbance. Researchers who studied the case noted that "deaths associated with other specialized diets have been reported," including liquid protein diets.

So on both sides of the calorie crisis—obesity at one extreme, radical dieting behaviors on the other—teens place themselves at risk for immediate diseases and/or for long-term illnesses. These ailments can damage teenagers' health at an early age and result in disability or premature death. Because they are young, growing rapidly, and undergoing vast hormonal change, teens are especially vulnerable to nutritional excesses and deficiencies, and can fall into avoidable disease processes that once initiated, may haunt them for a lifetime.

Chapter Five

Young people are inundated with images of the "perfect body." The mannequin displaying fashionable clothes in the foreground of this image has a very slender body type, but achieving that figure would be unhealthy for many teen girls.

Body Image, Extreme Dieting and the Media

At the emotional core of virtually every teenager are nagging questions about looks, attractiveness, and what social scientists call "body image." For many teens, body image becomes an obsession fueled by powerful forces all around them, including the mass media's projections of ideal physical beauty. A number of fashion magazines tout racy headlines about how to be physically enticing and improve specific areas of the body. Their photos and ads radiate beauty, trendiness, and startling thinness in girls. A similar body type is becoming the model for boys: male models appear in magazines with lean bodies and gaunt, chiseled faces. These images and their implicit messages mark the flipside of the obesity epidemic, in which thin masks an obsessive fear of fat and pushes teens toward embracing health dangers.

Although widely devoured and highly influential, magazine and media portrayals aren't alone in casting the cultural mold of body image. Often family members spell out the message years earlier. One teenager, Jan, told researchers J. Kevin Thompson and Linda Smolak that when she was only five years old her mother put her and her sister on a diet. Jan explained that her own mother is so sensitive about food issues that she "rarely eats in front of other people," a discomfort provoked by her own mother from an early age. Jan's grandmother "frequently makes comments about her daughter's weight." By the time Jan was 15, she was so terrified of becoming fat that she purged three times a day.

Jan and many girls like her are obsessed with weight and the rail-thin look they believe other people admire. They want to be thin because they see thin girls and women all around them on TV, in the movies, in magazines, on music videos, on the Internet, in product advertisements, and in clothing stores. In a 2003 Gallup poll that gathered information from teens ages 13 to 17 about their media usage habits, 11 percent said they watched more than 20 hours of television a week and nearly a third watched between 10 and 20 hours a week. Twenty-three percent of teens told Gallup in 2003 that a night of watching TV was their favorite after-school activity. Nine out of ten teens watched TV and listened to CDs or the radio every day. Many of the media images and lyrics teens encounter convey messages about sexual attraction and physical beauty.

Both boys and girls are strongly influenced by these images, according to Thompson and Smolak. Nearly half of girls as young as 14 years old and 20 percent of adolescent boys have reported trying to lose weight. The majority (55 percent) of girls and 35 percent of boys, the researchers found, were dissatisfied with their bodies, and a May 2000 Gallup survey found that most teens admitted being influenced by the media. Popular music was listed as an important influence by 72 percent of teens, while TV was an important influence for 49 percent of teens.

Other studies have shown the correlation between the media's portrayal of the ideal body and body image. In fact, 16 percent of girls and 12 percent of boys told researchers Jane Brown and Elizabeth Witherspoon "they had dieted or exercised to look like a television character," according to the *Journal of Adolescent Health.* Identifying with models or popular TV characters can strengthen

The media has a great influence on teens when it comes to body image. Studies show that young people want to emulate the physical characteristics of celebrities whose photos appear in magazines.

Teens were asked if they weighed more or less than they would like, or if they felt their weight was acceptable.

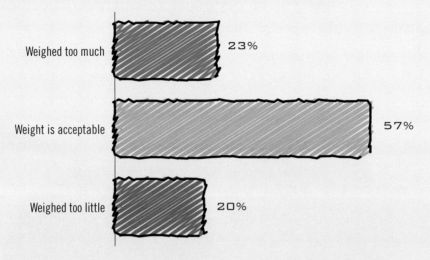

Weighed too much — 23%

Weight is acceptable — 57%

Weighed too little — 20%

Teens who said they weigh more than they would like said they tried to lose weight in the following ways (multiple responses were permitted):

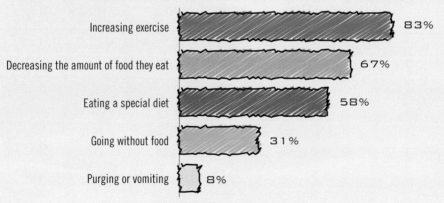

Increasing exercise — 83%

Decreasing the amount of food they eat — 67%

Eating a special diet — 58%

Going without food — 31%

Purging or vomiting — 8%

Poll taken January—March 1998; 500 total respondents age 13–17 answered the first question. Of that number, 116 teens responded to the second question.
Source: Gallup Youth Survey/The Gallup Organization.

the impact of body awareness, and a number of reports indicate that teens internalize the ideal thinness, imagining themselves in those bodies. After seeing images of thin models in one study, the authors found that "bulimic patients reported lower self-esteem and increased dissatisfaction with personal body weight." In 2001, more than half of teen girls told the Gallup Youth Survey that they would be "more pleased" about their appearance if they were thinner.

But cultural values and media portrayals of skinny people still represent only a piece of the larger story, say Thompson and Smolak. Being teased by friends, family, or schoolmates about being fat has a powerful impact on teen attitudes. Many teens are stung by their peers' comments about their bodies, their clothes, or their moral attitudes about sex. A Gallup Youth Survey in 2000 revealed that more than a third of teenagers were teased or taunted at school, and that teasing occured among boys slightly more than girls. Nearly half of the remarks concerned physical appearance. The majority of teens in this survey said their friends got teased or taunted, and 49 percent of boys and 36 percent of girls admitted to teasing or taunting others.

Alexander O. Eliot and Christina W. Baker, researchers at the Outpatient Eating Disorders Clinic at Boston Children's Hospital, reported that a 16-year-old boy diagnosed with anorexia nervosa traced his condition to an older sibling's teasing about his "chubbiness." When such humiliating remarks from friends or family combine with the flood of media images, teens long to be transformed. The media provides the false-ideal mirror on the wall while peers and family members provide the face-to-face humiliation.

"Perfect Bodies," Clinically Starving

Although the majority of teenagers are painfully self-conscious, most do not fall victim to eating disorders—at least not within the strict medical definitions of these conditions. However, many models and Hollywood actors who essentially set a standard for appearance fall within the body-weight criteria for eating disorders. Brown and Witherspoon report that models have gotten skinnier in recent years, and now weigh about 23 percent less than the average woman.

Even though teenage girls may feel anxious looking at images of women with far-from-average bodies, they still want to read magazines flooded with pictures of these models. Writing in the journal *Adolescence*, Steven R. Thomsen, Michelle Weber, and Lora Beth Brown reported that three out of four girls between ages 12 and 14 read beauty magazines, and that many of them have tried extreme dieting techniques. The frequency with which they read beauty magazines coincides with "weight loss practices that include using laxatives, taking weight control pills or appetite suppressants, skipping two meals a day, restricting caloric intake, or intentionally vomiting."

The physical effects of these practices can be devastating. Crash dieting, fasting, self-induced vomiting, skipped meals, and other forms of severe calorie reduction convey a false message to the body, telling the brain, fat cells, and crucial organs that the body is starving. One of many consequences is a slowing of metabolism to prevent starvation. In this metabolic state, the body preserves its stores of fat and imposes fatigue on the whole system to preserve calories for essential organs. Dieting ceases to be effective, and exercise becomes overwhelmingly exhausting. Moreover, when normal eating resumes, the body's slowed metabolism helps bring back the weight quickly. Two likely outcomes to this situation are more weight gain through yo-yo dieting or a spiral into malnutrition.

Boys Want to Be Strong and Wiry

Boys are also under increasing pressure to maintain ideal body image. According to Brown and Witherspoon, a recent study of male views suggests "an equally unattainable ideal image for men." In a review of eating disorder studies of boys, Aleixo M. Muise noted that teen males were "less concerned with exact

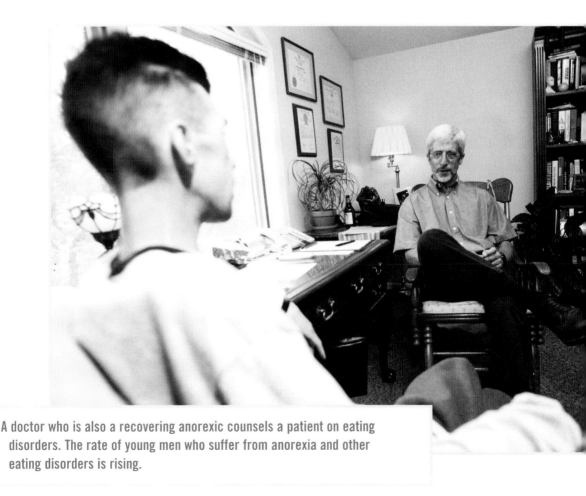

A doctor who is also a recovering anorexic counsels a patient on eating disorders. The rate of young men who suffer from anorexia and other eating disorders is rising.

weight or clothing size and more concerned with attaining an idealized masculine shape." The authors in this and other studies point to the recent trend of media portrayals of males "baring their carefully sculpted chests or chests devoid of any body fat." Social

A STORY OF AGONY

The following is a first-hand account of suffering from obesity, submitted to the American Obesity Association's website, obesity.org:

Hello. I live in Rochester, N.Y. I'm 17 years old and I weigh 440 pounds. I've been overweight since I was 12 years old. I used to go to school, but I had to drop out because people continued to make fun of me.

I suffer from depression, anxiety, and agoraphobia. I hate my body so much and I wish I could lose all this weight in a heartbeat, but I can't. Now I sit around in the house all day, and when I do go out I don't even get out of the car. I joined a gym, but I don't know what good that's going to do.

I missed my whole teenage-hood because of my obesity. I wish I could go to a store and buy sexy clothing and bell-bottoms and tank tops and a bikini, but I can't because they don't make clothing my size.

You know what, I feel so guilty for letting myself get so big and I wish I could just live an ordinary teenage life, and have cute boys look at me and not pick on me, because I would be beautiful. And I could go out and enjoy life instead of being afraid all the time.

I know I'm not the only obese person in the world but me being a teenager and watching all these other skinny teenage girls, it makes me feel like I am the only one and I feel like such a freak. I wish I could change, but it's so hard. I really need some support right now. I wish all these pretty, skinny, in-shape people could just respect me, but that will never happen because of the way I look.

scientists believe that this increased emphasis on idealized male stereotypes matches the long-standing portrayals of skinny females and likely increases the prevalence of body dissatisfaction among boys and men.

Writing for *Details* magazine, Peter Davis has described European male fashion models as "wisps with swizzle-stick arms and sunken chests." At Cornell University, being painfully skinny was so fashionable that a recent graduate said his fraternity was "a hotbed of anorexia." Davis dubbed the male version of the disease "manorexia" and attributed much of the trendy malnourished look to the emaciated frames of today's rock stars. According to the National Eating Disorders Association, male anorexia is on the rise and discontent over body image is a growing problem.

While boys are less frequently diagnosed with anorexia nervosa and bulimia than girls, they are nearly as likely to be identified with binge eating disorder. Once they reach levels of overweight or obesity, boys engage in bingeing or purging even more frequently than girls. Muise's report indicated that 20 percent of the boys in the studies were dieting, and of that number 7 percent were engaged in bingeing or purging. It also states, "These youths were also at greater risk to abuse alcohol and drugs and experience a range of psychological disturbances, including low self-esteem, depression, and [preoccupation with suicide]."

Many boys experience these pressures in the context of school sports. In one study of athletes diagnosed with eating or weight-related problems, more than a third of males were involved with an athletic team "in which weight control is important for good performance." According to Muise, many athletes fall prey to "over-exercising, prolonged fasting, vomiting, and the use of licit or illicit drugs such as laxatives, diuretics, steroids, or diet pills." These findings do not suggest that playing sports is bad. In fact, other studies indicate that sports improve relationships and academics, decrease depression, and provide the exercise that can prevent weight gain and its associated complications. However, the physical requirements of certain sports, such as wrestling, convince players to try crash-and-burn diets and ignore health dangers.

Problems of Self-Esteem

Generally, overweight children under eight and nine years of age do not suffer from diminished self-esteem, according to several studies reviewed by Thompson and Smolak. But soon weight consciousness emerges, and even some fourth and fifth graders begin expressing dissatisfaction with their bodies if they perceive themselves as overweight. Psychologists speculate that part of this pre-pubescent concern may reflect growing awareness of the negative social attitudes about being fat. This dissatisfaction eventually takes its toll on self-esteem as children grow older and face the complications of their own sexual attractiveness.

Negative self-esteem is a "significant predictor of eating disturbances," Thompson and Smolak conclude. Preoccupation with appearance can be even more pointed for an increasing number of teens with body dysmorphic disorder (BDD), defined by the American Psychiatric Association as "preoccupation with an imagined defect in appearance. If a slight physical anomaly is present, the person's concern is markedly excessive." Thompson and Smolak explain, "In other words, an objective observer might not discern evidence of an appearance problem, yet the young girl or boy is obsessed with the site of concern."

Most cases emerge in adolescence, and nine out of ten cases involve white females. A similar fixation marks a condition called body image disturbance (BID). According to researcher Rick M. Gardner, people who suffer with BID think they are fatter than they really are. They also don't like what they see in the mirror, finding fault with size, shape, and just about everything else.

Obesity, however, remains the fastest-growing weight-related condition. Its toll on self-esteem is often further damaged by a distorted self-image. "It takes an exceptionally strong adolescent to withstand the humiliation that often attaches to obese young people," write Andrea Marks and Betty Rothbart, authors of *Healthy Teens, Body and Soul*. Of course, no one deserves to be rejected for being overweight, and people of all body types and conditions should be treated with respect. Nevertheless, it must be recognized that obese adolescents are burdened by more than their excess pounds.

Teens who become obsessed with their weight constantly see themselves as larger than they are, and are often critical of their own appearance.

Chapter Six

Campers participate in an aerobics program at a weight-loss camp for young people in Pennsylvania. Participants at the camp come from throughout North America, spending up to eight weeks learning to lose weight through proper exercise and nutrition.

Combating Obesity

It has always been the case that children on average live longer than their parents, but health experts are concerned that if the obesity epidemic worsens, this norm will be reversed. Their greatest worry is over the worst complication of teen obesity: the onset of type II diabetes in young people by the age of 14. *Harvard Magazine* reports that type II diabetes reduces a person's life span by 17 to 29 years.

According to Steven Gortmaker of the Harvard School of Public Health, the serious consequences of obesity are the result of a small energy imbalance between food intake and physical activity — the "equivalent to the caloric content of one sugar-sweetened drink per day." Amazingly, scientists can measure the difference between an obesity epidemic and good national health as the equivalent of one can of soda a day — fewer than 200 calories.

However, caloric intake is only one of several measures of weight gain. In fact, adolescents ate fewer total calories in 1996 than in 1965, according to a 2000 study in the *Western Journal of Medicine.* It is the quality of those calories that makes a difference—increases in high-fat potatoes, pizza, macaroni and cheese, and sugared drinks have done much to off-set the reduced calories in teen diets. Moreover, the study report-ed, reductions in fruits, vegetables, fibers, and dairy products have led to crucial nutritional deficiencies that "may contribute to important increases in nutrition-related chronic diseases."

The real bottom line, however, is the decrease in teen activity. In 1965, teens were more physically active and burned off those extra calories. Today, only about 12 percent of 18-year-olds exercise enough to achieve cardiac fitness, reports Vicki L. Douthitt in an article for the *Journal of School Health.* According to the article, phys-ical activity declines by almost 50 percent during adolescence. Only a third of American school-age children meet even minimal fitness standards, and one out of five will "develop clinical symptoms of coronary heart disease before age 16," says Douthitt.

Frank Hu, a public health professor at the Harvard School of Public Health, stresses exercise in defeating obesity. "The single thing that comes close to a magic bullet, in terms of its strong and universal benefits, is exercise," says Hu. In fact, exercise trumps fat and weight in extending life expectancy. It is the best cure for over-weight, and for people genetically programmed to be obese; exer-cise even overcomes the negative effects of all those fat cells. People who are fat and fit live as long as people who are thin. Working out also improves health very rapidly and prevents chronic illness.

Exercise works in numerous important ways besides simply burning calories. Experts say that exercise can improve the structures in muscle cells that facilitate the burning of fat cells.

These improvements in turn increase resting metabolism. Unlike going on a diet, which often reduces metabolism and energy, exercise increases both, and if combined with only modest diet change can yield dramatic results. For most teens, regular exercise can eliminate any need for dieting and improve general health dramatically.

Exercise also acts directly on the mechanisms of overweight that cause mental sluggishness. A junk-food diet may result in depressed learning ability, according to a study of rats at California's Brain Injury Research Center. The rats that were fed a healthy diet and exercised regularly were able to memorize sections of a water maze; the junk-food rats swam around the pool randomly. Scientists have observed similar neurological factors that inhibit learning among overweight teens in Houston schools. In an article for *Reuters Health*, Amy Norton reported that problems in concentration in overweight students were attributed to high-fat diets and excessive junk food, and improved mental performance was the result of reducing junk food intake. Moreover, researchers have concluded that exercise stimulates the creation of new nerve cells. They liken exercise to mental fertilizer, growing and enriching brain cells.

Schools and Exercise Programs

Exercise may be the best way to maintain a healthy weight, but it is often difficult to convince kids to sustain their exercise programs over long periods. According to the CDC, nearly two-thirds of kids 9 to 13 years old "do not participate in any organized physical activity during non-school hours." Generally, teens are a bit more active than adults but much less active than their younger brothers and sisters.

TEACHING KIDS TO BE FIT

Who should teach children about weight issues?

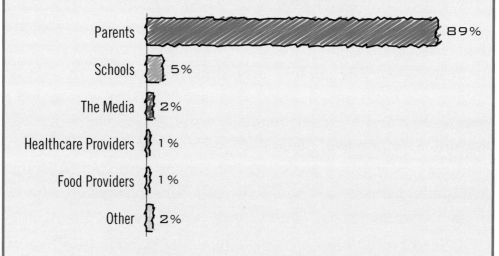

Parents	89%
Schools	5%
The Media	2%
Healthcare Providers	1%
Food Providers	1%
Other	2%

Who, besides parents, should teach children about weight issues?

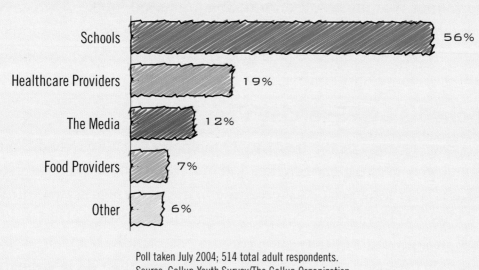

Schools	56%
Healthcare Providers	19%
The Media	12%
Food Providers	7%
Other	6%

Poll taken July 2004; 514 total adult respondents.
Source: Gallup Youth Survey/The Gallup Organization.

Douthitt reports that two-thirds of teens simply are not fit. To meet the CDC's exercise standards of good health, teens need 30 minutes of physical activity at least five times a week, or vigorous exercise for a minimum of 20 minutes at least three times a week. Only 7 percent of teens told Gallup that they exercise in the evening, so that leaves schools with the major task of promoting physical activity. In this area, most schools flunk outright.

Schools have reduced organized athletics and gym classes in recent years. A study released by the CDC in 2007 found that about 95 percent of American high schools had some physical education requirements, but only 2 percent of the schools provided daily gym class or its equivalent. Moreover, schools exempt up to 40 percent of students for various alternative activities, including other course work, community service, and vocational training.

Faced with these daunting numbers, many educators and health experts do not know how to begin to promote exercise, although nutritionist and pediatric physician James Hill found a new approach. He launched the Colorado on the Move program after discovering that on average Americans were only taking 5,500 steps in a day—not enough to prevent weight gain. Hill and his research team at the University of Colorado Nutrition Center believed that getting people to measure their activity was a start, so they handed out inexpensive pedometers to count steps. Hill reported that people enjoy counting and keeping score, and using the pedometer helps them set goals, one of which is to take 10,000 steps a day. Colorado schools began marching kids around during gym classes with pedometers. Even McDonald's jumped into the step-counting parade, offering pedometers with its new healthier alternative meals.

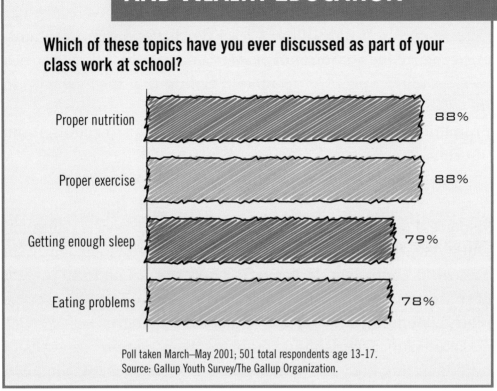

OBESITY, NUTRITION, AND HEALTH EDUCATION

Which of these topics have you ever discussed as part of your class work at school?

Topic	Percentage
Proper nutrition	88%
Proper exercise	88%
Getting enough sleep	79%
Eating problems	78%

Poll taken March–May 2001; 501 total respondents age 13-17.
Source: Gallup Youth Survey/The Gallup Organization.

Many gym programs only offer a slim set of choices for activities, and unsurprisingly, many students are not excited about gym class. For many students, competitive athletics are not much fun. Not everyone is driven to win games, and their demands on performing certain skills inhibit many teens, especially those who are shy and lack confidence. Moreover, few of these activities—offered only once or twice a week—come close to fulfilling CDC standards for vigorous activity. While a few teens benefit greatly from team sports, those who simply don't consider themselves athletes are largely neglected. Many of them are either overweight or vulnerable to becoming overweight because school gym classes are so limited. Can an activity like counting steps possibly be a fun alternative? The Colorado kids who used pedometers told the PBS news show *Frontline* they liked it, but their teachers lamented that offering one class of its kind per week was not nearly enough to be considered major progress.

What Works Is Also Fun

Social scientists and educators are trying to overcome the barriers that prevent teens from exercising. A crucial ingredient, not surprisingly, is that exercise should be fun. But what makes an activity fun? In an article for *Adolescence*, Randy Page and Larry Tucker concluded that teens who exercise frequently derive social enjoyment from their activities. When teens enjoy the company of exercise mates they also enjoy the exercise because serotonin levels in their brain have increased, giving them a sense of pleasure and relaxation during and after physical activity. Exercise and friendships thus reinforce each other while helping teens build social skills.

Those teens who say they don't enjoy exercise tend to be shy and feel "uncomfortable and inhibited in social settings," say Page and

In recent years doctors have encouraged people to "step up" the amount of walking they do. Pedometers like the one shown here record the number of steps taken each day; 10,000 steps daily is considered the minimum amount of healthy exercise.

Tucker. They also have lower self-esteem than those who regularly exercise. These negative emotions reinforce an aversion to exercise and sports, "resulting in a reluctance to participate in group exercise activities." This aversion in turn prevents the social contact that can make sports fun.

Other researchers have looked closely at additional personal barriers. Many teens say they are too fatigued or too depressed to exercise. Teens interviewed in a 2003 study published in *Physical Educator* said they lacked transportation or facilities. Others said they lacked confidence in their abilities, but the most common excuse was a "lack of time." Given the amount of time teens watch TV, this answer was too easy and really not true, the researchers said. Among girls, lack of an exercise partner was often cited, as was the excuse that "exercise is boring." Moreover, exercise for some teens is costly or too embarrassing, requiring them to dress in "clothes that look funny." Beyond that, exercise is "too tiring" for some teens.

According to proponents of an exercise campaign known as VERB, run by the CDC, the emphasis for girls should be less on social activities and more on activities that yield a high success rate of body change. These include walking, jogging, weight training, cycling, dance, step aerobics, and tennis. "Female adolescents are concerned about their bodies, and activities such as these will de-emphasize competition and emphasize individual body changes as they occur," says the CDC. Girls are also motivated by gain in athletic competency, physical appearance, and self-worth, says Douthitt.

One of the key motivating factors that Douthitt found for boys to exercise is the perceived gain in "romantic appeal" that comes with being fit and strong. But activities in gym classes don't meet these goals particularly well, with their emphasis on team sports. Some schools are taking a very hard look at the usual selection of gym activities and are trying to make classes more varied. According to a 2001 PBS *NewsHour* special, "Schools across the country are trying to make gym class more fun by adding activities like rollerblading, rock climbing or treadmill running." Whatever activities that teens decide upon, exercise works. The *British Journal of Sports Medicine* recommends programs that include both aerobic exercise and weight training. The latter form of exercise not only reduces fat but increases "fat-free mass," which in turn increases metabolism.

Many researchers agree that teens need support from friends, family, and teachers for these programs to work. They must set realistic goals, have fun, participate with friends, reward each other with praise, and work hard enough for a good sweat. The rewards are remarkable, however, in the short run and for a lifetime. According to Melinda Sothern of the Louisiana Childhood Obesity Laboratory, a mix of modest dietary change and exercise can not only reverse teen obesity but can also prevent the onset of adult obesity.

Diets and Nutrition

Most diet and exercise schemes fail because they are too ambitious, too dramatic, and thus too difficult to pursue. The old adage of "No pain, no gain" may work for a few weeks, but the best remedies are gradual and comfortably absorbed into daily routines. Because teens' bodies are growing and changing, both diet and exercise need to be maintained in a safe manner. Dieting schemes that are extremely difficult cause intense cravings, painful hunger, fatigue, irritability, or binge eating. More importantly, they slow metabolism and will simply not work over time. The most effective diet and exercise programs must be able to be folded painlessly into lifestyle and become a permanent and enjoyable part of life.

Fasting is the worst of all dieting approaches. Many experts suggest that to lose a pound a week (the maximum safe target), most teens need to reduce 500 calories daily by cutting back on food and increasing exercise.

For two decades, the U.S. Department of Agriculture (USDA) used a pyramid-shaped chart to illustrate the requirements of a healthful daily diet. The Food Guide Pyramid was divided into six food groups and listed the recommended number of daily servings from each group. At the base of the pyramid was the bread, cereal, rice, and pasta group; the USDA recommended that people eat 6–11 servings from this group each day. Directly above the bread, cereal, rice, and pasta group were the vegetable group (3–5 servings) and fruit group (2–4 servings). Above them were the milk, yogurt, and cheese group (2–3 servings) and the meat, poultry, fish, dry beans, eggs, and nuts group (2–3 servings). At the top of the pyramid were fats, oils, and sweets, which the USDA advised should be consumed sparingly.

The Food Guide Pyramid had its critics. Some said it was a bit

(continued on page 90)

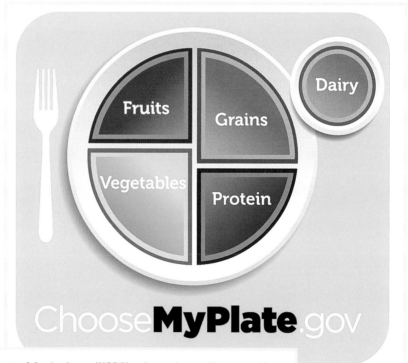

In 2011, the U.S. Department of Agriculture (USDA) released new dietary guidelines for Americans, which recommend eating healthy foods such as vegetables, fruits, whole grains, fat-free and low-fat dairy products, and seafood while consuming less sodium, saturated and trans fats, added sugars, and refined grains. More information on healthy eating can be found at the USDA website, www.choosemyplate.gov.

FINDING A GOOD EXERCISE PROGRAM

Designing an effective activity program is simpler than eating well but requires time, commitment, and organization. Participants in a study known as the National Weight Control Registry, which tracks dieters who lost at least 30 pounds for a year or more, exercise enough to burn 400 calories a day—the equivalent to an hour's brisk walk. The key to exercise is to keep pushing a little harder as the days and weeks pass. It does not need to hurt, but sweating and breathing hard are signals that the activity is beneficial.

Time for an Average 150 lb. Adult to Burn 150 Calories

Intensity	Activity	METs	Duration
Moderate	Volleyball, noncompetitive	3.0	43
Moderate	Walking, moderate pace (3 mph, 20 min/mile)	3.5	37
Moderate	Walking, brisk pace (4 mph, 15 min/mile)	4.0	32
Moderate	Table tennis	4.0	32
Moderate	Raking leaves	4.5	32
Moderate	Social dancing	4.5	29
Moderate	Lawn mowing (powered push mower)	4.5	29
Hard	Jogging (5 mph, 12 min/mile)	7.0	18
Hard	Field hockey	8.0	16
Very hard	Running (6 mph, 10 min/mile)	10.0	13

Source: *Surgeon General's Report on Physical Activity and Health,* 1996.

The federal standard calls for 30 minutes of moderate activity each day or vigorous activity three days a week. Moderate activity can be "sustained relatively comfortably for a long period of time (about 60 minutes)," according to the American Council on Exercise. It should cause an elevation in heart and breathing rates but not prevent people from talking comfortably as they exercise. Vigorous exercise three times a week should be intense enough to raise heart and breathing rates. For most people this level of exercise lasts "about 20 minutes before fatigue sets in," the council says. Either vigorous exercise, light activity, or some combination of both will work to improve health and prevent weight gain. At left is a chart measuring activities of varying intensities and the amount of energy and time they require. One MET, or metabolic equivalent, is the amount of energy used when sitting quietly.

Harvard researchers advocate endurance training for the heart; resistance (strength) training to increase muscle capacity and metabolism; and flexibility training for joint health and muscle range. Resistance training usually involves weights or exercise machines with repetitive movements in sets of eight to a dozen until the movement becomes difficult. The goal is to strengthen muscle groups, adding repetitions until the motion becomes easy (12 to 15 reps) and then moving on to greater resistance. Many health clubs have personal trainers to help people get started on a program. Exercise machines tend to be safer than free weights if used properly because the movements are guided and can be more easily controlled.

The American Council on Exercise suggests dozens of different ways to achieve cardiac fitness, from walking to setting up a home gym to joining a health club. The keys are motivation and persistence. Inhibiting factors may be cost and time. "Exercising at home can be more economical than exercising at a health club," the council says. "Invest in a good pair of running or walking shoes, some adjustable dumbbells and an exercise mat, and you're ready to go. For some people, the best part of home exercise is the privacy." Home machines such as stationary bikes, treadmills, steppers, resistance gyms, and the like can be used watching TV, reading, or listening to music to reduce boredom. But many people can't discipline themselves at home, so opting for a health club, going with a friend, or using school facilities can be an important motivator.

difficult to use. How much food, for example, constituted a serving? Other critics claimed the USDA panel that set the dietary guidelines was heavily influenced by lobbying from industry groups such as the American Meat Institute and the National Cattlemen's Beef Association. It was well established, after all, that a diet heavy in fatty red meat raises cholesterol and the risk of heart disease. As protein sources, lean meat, fish, nuts, or beans are more healthful alternatives. Yet the Food Guide Pyramid did not reflect this reality, and some people might eat two or three servings of red meat every day and believe they were maintaining a good diet. Similarly, the bread, cereal, rice, and pasta group did not distinguish between refined grains and whole grains. The latter are much more healthful.

In 2011, the USDA responded to such criticisms by replacing the pyramid with another graphic representation of nutrition guidelines. Called MyPlate, it's a simple place setting, depicted from above. At the left of the colorful icon is a fork. Next to it is a circular plate divided into four sections: grains (covering about 30 percent of the plate), protein (20 percent), vegetables (30 percent), and fruits (20 percent). A smaller circle to the right of the plate represents a glass and is labeled dairy. Accompanying MyPlate are recommendations that urge people, among other things, to control portion size, reduce salt and sugar in their diet, switch to low-fat or skim milk, make at least half of the grains they eat whole grains, and vary their protein sources.

In introducing MyPlate, First Lady Michelle Obama—who'd made good nutrition and exercise for kids one of her primary focuses—touted the new guidelines' simplicity. "Parents don't have the time to measure out exactly three ounces of chicken or to look up how much rice or broccoli is in a serving. . . . And we're all bombarded with so many dietary messages that it's hard to find time to sort through all this information," Mrs. Obama said. "But we do have time to take a look at our kids' plates. We do it all the time. . . . And as long as they're eating proper portions, as long as half of their meal is fruits and vegetables alongside their lean proteins, whole grains and low-fat dairy, then we're good."

The Calorie Question

Many nutritionists say that the path to reduced calories begins by diligently keeping track of caloric gain and loss. For example, a sensible plan to reduce 500 calories per day may begin by substituting a glass of water for a soda (150 fewer calories) and walking for 30 minutes (the walking need not be continuous or at one time but can be split up throughout the day). The walking will burn 150 calories, yielding a total reduction of 300 calories. The following activities, given by Coolnurse.com, also are effective calorie-burners: a game of basketball for 30 minutes burns nearly 300 calories; weight training, about 250 calories; raking the yard, about 100; mowing the lawn, about 300. Bowling for an hour and a half burns about 400 calories. A half-hour of fast dancing burns about 200 calories; about the same is burned while riding a bike at a relaxed 10 miles per hour. Swimming or cross-country skiing burns 400 calories or more in a half-hour.

Nutritionist Erin Pammer recommends that rather than paying such close attention to calories, people simply pay closer attention to their own body signals—eating when hungry and stopping when full. She suggests that people "enjoy foods that are high in calories and fat," but eat them less frequently and in smaller portions. The refrigerator should be filled with healthy, appealing foods, and people should enjoy them. She urges people to "forget dieting," but instead to eat more slowly and be more conscious of the pleasure of eating food.

Dangers of Magic Pills

The magic pills and miracle products offered by supplement makers should be avoided, warn experts. The supplement industry is virtually unregulated in the United States, and the FDA has been very slow in ordering the removal from store shelves of supplements that are known to be dangerous, according to a *Consumer Reports* investigation. One such supplement, ephedra, was ordered off the market by the FDA in 2004, though products containing ephedra can still be purchased on the Internet. *Consumer Reports* says that supplement makers have begun replacing ephedra with other stimulants such as a product known as bitter orange, which the magazine's researchers consider "likely hazardous" and among the most dangerous supplements.

Many manufacturers make extravagant claims for diet products. While advertising claims are supposed to be truthful, the diet industry is often unable to resist the temptation of enticing customers with clever come-ons that are too good to be true. One website claims its product will yield "incredible weight loss" without resorting to "crash diets or strenuous exercise." The website touts the product's "all natural" ingredients and "amazing, safe formula" but one of the ingredients is the controversial bitter orange. Diet pills sold as supplements are not regulated or tested under the same laws governing medicinal drugs, and many are potentially dangerous. Touting products as natural does not necessarily mean they are harmless. Many hazardous medicines are natural, as are many poisons.

Get Moving

In reaction to the alarming increase in overweight and obesity in the United States, First Lady Michelle Obama launched "Let's Move!" The initiative focuses on helping young people eat better and exercise more.

While the results of taking such steps are less immediate, they are proven to be more effective than a vast majority of most

Education about the importance of good nutrition has become more widespread in recent years. First Lady Michelle Obama has made an effort to teach people about proper nutrition and and the benefits of exercise for young people.

commercial diet plans. Not only do many weight loss schemes fail, they also ultimately lead to weight gain, according to scientific research. A 1999 NIMH study conducted by the American Psychological Association found that robust weight-reduction schemes backfire. "The most striking finding was that elevated dieting and radical weight-loss efforts predicted . . . an elevated hazard for the onset of obesity," the report revealed. Failed diets may just be brief episodes in a lifelong trend of weight gain. One physiological explanation of this trend is that

RYAN'S STORY

At 14 years old, five feet nine, 271 pounds, and with a body mass index of 40, Ryan is obese, but he doesn't really feel that way. He is very active and is involved in the martial arts, falconry, trail riding, and he works out on a home Total Gym several times a week. Like many teens, he is very busy with schoolwork, but in an interview, Ryan stated that he is very active at least four hours a day.

Weight became an issue for Ryan when he was about nine years old and he and his mother were taking lots of trips through the fast-food drive-thru window. But he's now sick of fast food and has learned how to cook and enjoy healthy meals. He confesses that he's not a great veggie fan and likes potatoes "in every form," as well as steak, chicken, rice, and burgers. Neither he nor his mother considers him an especially big eater, and he does not binge.

But Ryan drinks three to four 12-ounce sodas a day, and he's probably inherited fat genes from both sides of his family. Although his mother has never had a weight problem, her mother has struggled with weight her whole adult life. Ryan's father, once skinny, has been gaining weight, and he comes from an obese family. Ryan may struggle with weight his whole life, but he enjoys working out, and learning about good food and diet may help him beat the odds. So far he is healthy and likes the feeling of being fit.

metabolism slows down during dieting and the body adjusts to living on fewer calories. The rapid weight loss only makes the body increasingly resistant to weight-loss schemes.

Researchers at the Harvard School of Public Health (HSPH) have made similar conclusions about crash dieting. They even recommend against dieting of any kind for normal-weight teens. "Although medically supervised diets may be helpful and appropriate for overweight youth, our data suggest that for many adolescents, dieting to control weight is not only ineffective, it may actually promote weight gain," say the researchers of the Harvard Diet and Adolescent Obesity Project.

Low-Carb Craze Questioned

The low-carb diet craze, initiated by the Atkins Diet in the late 1990s, includes plenty of fat, even bacon, yet excludes bread, potatoes, pasta, and high-carb foods once thought essential to a balanced diet. The low-carb craze has swept the food industry in recent years. Unfortunately, according to an investigation by *Consumer Reports*, manufacturers do not always tell the truth about the low-carb foods they tout in ads and on labels. According to the report, many food companies list "net carbs" on their labels, which subtract the content of sugar alcohols and processed corn fibers that are used as substitutes for real sugar and starches. The substitute ingredients do not elevate blood sugar as much as sugar or conventional carbohydrates, but they contain nearly as many calories as regular food and are likely to fool people into thinking they will lose weight because they are eating fewer conventional carbohydrates. If they are eating as many or more calories, however, they will not lose weight because calories determine weight gain more than any other factor.

The low-fat diet craze of the 1980s and 1990s created a similar buzz that actually led to a 6 percent reduction of fat in the American diet. Nonetheless, people generally became fatter anyway since many of the most popular low-fat foods had just as many calories and many were snacks and desserts. Because they knew they were eating less fat, people ate more of these comfort foods than they should have, actually increasing calories and eliminating the benefit of eating less fat. The low-carb diet craze has produced similar results by encouraging many dieters to eat more fat than they should because they think they are eating fewer calories.

Studies of popular low-carb diets have shown that they do reduce pounds, owing to the fewer calories people eat during the diet. The high volumes of protein, moreover, do not set off steep spikes in insulin as sugars and refined starches do, thus making dieters feel more satisfied and fuller after their meals. However, a year or so after beginning the diet, many people gain their weight back at the same rate and frequency as with other diet plans.

Like any diet, to succeed a low-carb diet must be accompanied by increased exercise and permanent changes in lifestyle. In addition, scientists warn that the consumption of all the fat that a diet like Atkins permits may be dangerous. In 2009, the NIH published the results of a five-year study of low-carb diets, and found that they were about as effective as other diets at aiding weight loss. The key to weight loss, reported the NIH, was reducing the overall intake of calories, not whether the diet was high in protein or low in fat.

Drug Therapy

For morbidly obese teens—those who are dangerously over-weight—more aggressive treatments may be required. One approach has been to combine drug therapies with behavioral counseling linked to diet. Sibutramine, a drug that improves retention and production of serotonin and dopamine—another hormone connected with the pleasure system—was given to a group of obese adolescents who were placed on a restrictive diet of 1,200 to 1,500 calories per day. They met frequently for group discussions with dietary experts and psychotherapists, and their parents met separately with the experts for coaching on how to help. The drug had the effect of reducing appetite and hunger symptoms, and the therapy sessions helped motivate and inform the participants. After 12 months, the average weight lost was 17.2 pounds, according to the study's lead author, Dr. Robert Berkowitz. This decrease was more than double the loss for a control group not taking the drugs. Unfortunately, sibutramine also causes blood pressure and pulse increases among many people. Treatments using the drug are currently considered experimental and must be conducted under close supervision.

Another drug, metformin, has been used for treatment of type II diabetes and also promotes weight loss. It has been used in several small studies for weight reduction. While the drug is effective, its side effects, which include possible liver and kidney damage, concern patients and doctors.

For some obese adolescents with deficiencies in leptin—the hormone that tells the brain to decrease appetite—leptin infusions have been effective in reducing fat. However, not all obese people have this deficiency in their genes. For obese teens with normal leptin secretions, increasing hormone levels is not likely to be effective. In the meantime, the infusions and the drug therapies are subject to further research.

Cosmetic and Stomach-Reduction Surgery

Cosmetic surgery has mushroomed in recent years in the adult population, and one important target has been fat. According to researcher David B. Sarwer, 175,000 adolescents were surgically treated in 1999, and liposuction (fat removal) has been growing as an alternative to dieting. Typically, as Sarwer's case of a 17-year-old named Jessica illustrates, adolescents are pursuing what they see as last efforts to lose weight. A high school graduate, Jessica wanted liposuction to remove fat on her hips and thighs that made her feel self-conscious in summer clothes and swimsuits. Before seeking surgery, she dieted and exercised, losing 15 pounds, but remained uncomfortable about her appearance. The surgery reduced her discomfort, she said.

The most radical treatment for obesity is stomach-reduction surgery, but it is also risky and considered a treatment of last resort. According to the *Boston Globe,* there are "powerful indications that doctors increasingly see surgery as an option for obese children." Tufts University in Boston has been a pioneer in exploring surgery for adolescents. The procedure (also called bariatric or gastric bypass surgery) involves blocking most of the stomach from being able to hold food by stapling it shut. What is left is a tiny pouch the size of a small apple that initially holds only about an ounce of food, only a fraction of the 64-ounce (half-gallon) capacity of a normal stomach. The intestine is then cut from its position at the lower part of the stomach and re-attached to the pouch, bypassing the big part of the stomach.

While surgeons are getting better at the procedure, it is still very risky, with up to a 20 percent chance of complications and a death rate of nearly 1 percent, according to the American Obesity

Association. Life after the surgery is also a considerable challenge. Patients must eat numerous small meals and comply with a strict diet. However, they do feel less hungry, as was the case with Amy, a young woman whose stomach-reduction surgery was shown on the PBS television series *Scientific American Frontiers*. Interviewed several months after the procedure, she said, "I don't have that pit in my stomach like, Oh my gosh, I'm so hungry, I need to eat. Nothing like what it used to be. Nothing at all," she said. However, given enough time, those who undergo the procedure can eventually stretch that little pouch by overeating and begin to gain their weight back.

Because the risk is high and strict compliance essential, doctors

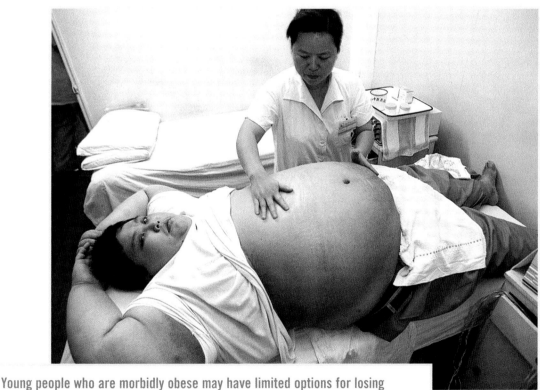

Young people who are morbidly obese may have limited options for losing weight. In some cases, surgery or other drastic treatments may be required.

choose adolescent patients very carefully. Dr. Brian Gilchrist, chief of Tufts–New England Medical Center pediatric surgery unit, says, "These kids sit in my office, and the tears roll down their cheeks. They suffer. There is tremendous prejudice," he told the *Boston Globe*. But the doctors have to look at school attendance and behavior to make sure candidates for the surgery are disciplined enough to persevere and succeed.

After completing the stomach surgery on 33 teenagers, Virginia physician Harvey Sugerman revealed that some patients suffered complications, "including four teenagers who had wound infections and six who developed hernias." Also, half of them regained all their weight after 10 years, Sugerman told the *Globe*. However, many fared very well afterwards, with eight getting married and having children, five finishing college, and most feeling better about themselves. While the number of stomach-reduction surgeries for adolescents probably only stands in the low thousands now, it is growing rapidly.

For anyone to take such a risk would seem, on its surface, to be foolhardy, a complete surrender to overeating and utter collapse of will. But the truth is that many of the people who have reached this stage of fat have tried every diet in the books. They've exercised, counted calories, deprived themselves for months, lost weight, and always gained it back. In an interview for *Scientific American Frontiers*, Dr. Jeffrey Friedman said that most people can function pretty well if they're 15 or 20 pounds overweight. They can lose that weight and will probably fluctuate up and down around that range for a very long time. But he explains that to lose more than 15 to 20 pounds "it becomes increasingly difficult because, to a greater extent, as more weight has to be lost, the biological drives that resist" weight loss "get more and more potent." When people reach the point that they're 100 or 200 pounds overweight, "it's exceedingly difficult and may even be impossible for the vast majority of people."

Unlike quitting smoking, which many teen smokers believe they can and sometimes do immediately, losing a large amount of excess fat is always a long process. There is no quitting "cold turkey" with food. Moreover, the health consequences of obesity are just as bad as those of cigarettes.

For most people today, being fat is no longer protective or useful. Yet it remains a vestige of human survival that has not shrunken but bloomed, finding ideal conditions in a society of plentiful resources. Eating, one of the most powerful human drives, is today indulged by an abundance of food beyond the wildest dreams of ancient people who were burdened by hard physical labor and hunger. The challenge for teens is to see the perils of this abundance.

It seems appropriate that although the obesity issue is extremely complex, a simple solution is available. Exercise and good nutritional habits sustain the body and, for the overwhelming majority of people, erase fat as a health concern. More Americans now know that failure to follow such modest steps may push them further toward a point of no return, with obesity possibly becoming the greatest preventable cause of premature death in the United States.

Glossary

BLOOD PRESSURE—the force of blood against the arterial walls produced by the pumping of the heart; high blood pressure (hypertension) increases risk of heart attacks or strokes.

BODY MASS INDEX (BMI)—a measure of fat in the total body as related to height and weight; results indicate levels of weight from underweight to obesity.

CALORIE—a unit of heat used to measure the potential energy in food.

CARBOHYDRATES—one of the primary food groups that include starches, sugars, and fibers from breads, cereals, potatoes, rice, pasta, fruit, and vegetables.

CHOLESTEROL—waxy substance found throughout the body, blood, and organs that is produced in the liver and ingested via food derived from animals.

DIABETES—serious life-long disease resulting from improper production or use of insulin to break down food for use by the body. Type II diabetes usually starts in adolescence or later, triggered or aggravated by poor diet and lack of exercise.

EATING DISORDER—medical condition characterized by repeated abnormal eating or dieting behaviors such as bingeing, fasting, and purging.

GENES—tiny strings of molecules in cells that contain the blueprints for all cell behavior and growth.

GLUCOSE—basic energy fuel that is produced from carbohydrates during digestion, transported by blood, and converted by insulin for use in muscles and organs.

HEART DISEASE—condition including several disorders that impair heart function, the most common of which is clogged heart arteries resulting from high cholesterol, poor diet, and lack of exercise.

INSULIN—hormone produced and secreted by the pancreas that unlocks glucose for use by muscles and organs.

LEPTINS—hormones that carry chemical signals between tissues and the brain regulating appetite and energy.

Glossary

METABOLISM—the intricate process of burning calories to produce energy required for life and movement.

MORBID OBESITY—state of being 50 percent or 100 pounds above ideal body weight; dangerously overweight.

OBESITY—state of being 20 to 25 percent above ideal weight; significantly overweight.

OVERWEIGHT—state of being 20 or more pounds above ideal weight.

PEDIATRIC—relating to a branch of medicine that focuses upon adolescents and children.

PHYSIOLOGICAL—relating to a human body's normal functioning.

SEDENTARY—characterized by limited movement, sitting, or resting; the opposite of active.

SEROTONIN—chemical transmitter in the brain affecting mood, emotion, pleasure, and appetite.

SUPPLEMENT—any vitamin, mineral, herb, botanical, extract, or chemical synthesis of these substances that is not subject to FDA medicine testing.

Internet Resources

http://www.gallup.com

Visitors to the Internet site maintained by the Gallup Organization can find results of Gallup Youth Surveys as well as many other research projects undertaken by the national polling firm.

http://www.diabetes.org

This comprehensive site of the American Diabetes Association includes research information, educational materials, and patient support.

http://www.cdc.gov/healthyweight/assessing/bmi/index.html

Anyone can use the BMI (body mass index) calculator at this site by typing in his or her height and weight.

http://www.coolnurse.com

A remarkably thorough, candid, and teen-friendly site with an extensive archive of articles on teen health and diet. Volunteer nurses who really know their audience manage this page.

http://www.mayoclinic.com/health/obesity/DS00314

The Mayo Clinic offers a clear, easy-to-read medical exploration of obesity and eating disorders by the staff of a highly respected hospital.

http://www.nationaleatingdisorders.org

This comprehensive site of the National Association of Eating Disorders provides research, education, programs, self-help, support, and advocacy.

Internet Resources

http://www.usda.gov

The official dietary word from the U.S. government sprawls outward with links to many organizations and publications.

http://www.choosemyplate.gov

The website for the government's Choose My Plate initiative, which aims to educate parents about the benefits of proper nutrition. The page includes links to many resources.

http://www.letsmove.gov

Let's Move! is a comprehensive initiative launched by First Lady Michelle Obama that is dedicated to solving the challenge of childhood obesity.

Further Reading

Brownell, Kelly D., and Katherine B. Horgen. *Food Fight*. New York: McGraw-Hill, 2003.

Bashe, Philip. *The Complete and Authoritative Guide for Caring for Your Teenager*. New York: Bantam Books, 2003.

Kessler, David A. *Your Food Is Fooling You: How Your Brain Is Hijacked by Sugar, Fat and Salt*. New York: Roaring Brook Press, 2012.

Koplewicz, Harold S. *More Than Moody: Recognizing and Treating Adolescent Depression*. New York: G. P. Putnam's Sons, 2002.

Marks, Andrea, and Betty Rothbart. *Healthy Teens, Body and Soul*. New York: Simon & Schuster, 2003.

Shell, Ellen R. *The Hungry Gene: The Science of Fat and the Future of Thin*. New York: Atlantic Monthly Press, 2002.

Taubes, Gary. *Why We Get Fat and What to Do About It*. New York: Anchor Books, 2011.

Willett, Walter. *Eat, Drink, and Be Healthy*. New York: Simon & Schuster, 2001.

Index

Numbers in **bold italic** refer to captions and graphs.

Index

Index

Index

Picture Credits

Contributors

GEORGE GALLUP JR. (1930–2011) was involved with The Gallup Organization for more than 50 years. He served as chairman of The George H. Gallup International Institute and served on many boards involved with health, educa- tion, and religion, including the Princeton Religion Research Center, which he co-founded.

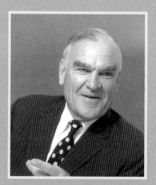

Mr. Gallup was internationally recognized for his research and study on youth, health, religion, and urban problems. He wrote numerous books, including *My Kids On Drugs?* with Art Linkletter (Standard, 1981); *The Great American Success Story* with Alec Gallup and William Proctor (Dow Jones-Irwin, 1986); *Growing Up Scared in America* with Wendy Plump (Morehouse, 1995); *Surveying the Religious Landscape: Trends in U.S. Beliefs* with D. Michael Lindsay (Morehouse, 1999); and *The Next American Spirituality* with Timothy Jones (Chariot Victor Publishing, 2002).

Mr. Gallup received his BA degree from the Princeton University Department of Religion in 1954, and held seven honorary degrees. He received many awards, including the Charles E. Wilson Award in 1994, the Judge Issacs Lifetime Achievement Award in 1996, and the Bethune-DuBois Institute Award in 2000. Mr. Gallup passed away in November 2011.

THE GALLUP YOUTH SURVEY was founded in 1977 by Dr. George Gallup to pro- vide ongoing information on the opinions, beliefs and activities of America's high school students and to help society meet its responsibility to youth. The topics examined by the Gallup Youth Survey have covered a wide range— from abortion to zoology. From its founding through the year 2001, the Gallup Youth Survey sent more than 1,200 weekly reports to the Associated Press, to be distributed to newspapers around the nation.

DR. PETER OWENS earned his masters and doctorate in education at Harvard University and is a writing professor at the University of Massachusetts Dartmouth. He is the author of *Oil and Chemical Spills,* a nonfiction book for young adults, and *Rips,* a novel. He is a widely published and award-winning journalist, software designer, and founder of KidNews.com.